"I was goi..."

"But you *didn't*."

His face twisted with an agony that broke her heart, and she reached out, touching his chest with her hands. The beating of his heart was under her palms, and all she wanted to do was take away the pain.

"For God's sake, lady, run," Jake whispered. "Now."

"No." The single word stood between them; then she felt his hold on her ease.

His hands shifted, touching her neck, but this time there was no threat in them. His fingers trembled on her skin, and he whispered, "You're so delicate. So vulnerable. I never wanted to hurt you. I never..."

Whitney touched her finger to his lips. "I know. I understand."

His lids lowered, his gaze shadowy, but the edge of pain was there. "No, you don't," he breathed hoarsely. "*I* don't even understand it."

Dear Reader,

Hot weather, hot books. What could be better? This month, Intimate Moments starts off with an American Hero to remember in Kathleen Korbel's *Simple Gifts*. This award-winning author has—as usual!—created a book that you won't be able to put down. You also might have noticed that the cover of this particular book looks a little bit different from our usual. We'll be doing some different things with some of our covers from time to time, and I hope you'll keep your eye out for that. Whenever you see one of our out-of-the-ordinary covers, you can bet the book will be out of the ordinary, too.

The month keeps going in fine form, with *Flynn*, the next installment of Linda Turner's tremendously popular miniseries, "The Wild West." Then check out *Knight's Corner*, by Sibylle Garrett, and *Jake's Touch*, by Mary Anne Wilson, two authors whose appearances in the line are always greeted with acclaim. Finally, look for two authors new to the line. Suzanne Brockmann offers *Hero Under Cover*, while Kate Stevenson gives you *A Piece of Tomorrow*.

I'd also like to take this chance to thank those of you who've written to me, sharing your opinions of the line. Your letters are one of my best resources as I plan for the future, so please feel free to keep letting me know what you think about the line and what you'd like to see more of in the months to come.

As always—enjoy!

Leslie Wainger
Senior Editor and Editorial Coordinator

Please address questions and book requests to:
Reader Service
U.S.: P.O. Box 1325, Buffalo, NY 14269
Canadian: P.O. Box 1050, Niagara Falls, Ont. L2E 7G7

JAKE'S TOUCH

Mary Anne Wilson

Silhouette®
INTIMATE MOMENTS®

Published by Silhouette Books

America's Publisher of Contemporary Romance

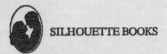

SILHOUETTE BOOKS

ISBN 0-373-07574-X

JAKE'S TOUCH

MARY ANNE WILSON

fell in love with reading at ten years of age, when she discovered *Pride and Prejudice*. A year later she knew she had to be a writer when she found herself writing a new ending for *A Tale of Two Cities*. A true romantic, she had Sydney Carton rescued, and he lived happily ever after.

Though she's a native of Canada, she now lives in California with her husband, a six-toed black cat who believes he's Hungarian and five timid Dobermans, who welcome any and all strangers. And she's writing happy endings for her *own* books.

For Walker Scott,
with lots of love

Prologue

June 30th, Washington, D.C.

Whitney Tate had felt uneasy all day, partly because she hated thunderstorms and one was building to a crescendo over the city. And partly because she had an ominous feeling that something was going to happen. Worse yet, she didn't have an idea what that "something" was.

A few minutes before five o'clock, she sat alone in her office on the tenth floor of the Madison Building just off Pennsylvania Avenue. With her back to her cluttered desk, she stared out the curtainless windows. She cringed as lightning ripped through the darkening skies, and for a moment her reflection was exposed in the rain-spattered glass by the white flash.

The image was smeared by the rain streaking the windowpane. Her feathery cap of wheat-blond hair, which had begun to curl slightly from the humidity, looked a bit like a halo. But there was nothing ethereal about the uneasiness that touched her wide-set blue eyes or the expression on her pale lips. As the lightning died and thunder rumbled in the distance, her image was gone, fading away like a ghost.

"Whitney?"

She jumped at the unexpected sound of someone saying her name, and she swiveled her wooden chair around to find a man standing in the open door of her office. A real ghost. He came from her past, a past she thought she'd put behind her well over a year ago.

In a rain-darkened trench coat, Cutter Ford looked as average as he always had. Average height, average weight, average coloring, the usual briefcase in his hand. The man could blend into any crowd...at least, until someone looked into his eyes.

She didn't know anyone who looked into those green eyes without having a split second of uneasiness, wondering if the man was looking into their souls. A foolish notion, but one Whitney had never been able to shake.

"What are you doing here, Cutter?" she asked, faintly pleased that her voice didn't give away the shock she felt at his sudden appearance.

As he stepped into the room, he swung the door shut with one hand, then swiped at his damp, sandy-blond hair. "You once told me that you owed me for pulling strings to let you get out of your old position and get hired on here."

The uneasiness she had been trying to fight all day finally had a name. Cutter Ford. She swallowed a bitterness that rose in the back of her throat. "What's this all about?"

"I'm pulling in my marker." He laid his briefcase on her cluttered desk, either not noticing or not caring that he was crushing her papers under the damp leather.

The past had reared its ugly head, and Whitney was clasping her hands so tightly together that they were tingling. "You helped me out when I needed it, that's true."

He undid the buttons on his coat without looking away from Whitney, his green eyes unblinking. "Now I need you for a job."

She couldn't have heard him right. "Cutter, I'm not working for you anymore. That was the whole idea—"

He leaned forward, pressing the tips of his fingers to the leather of his closed briefcase and cutting off her words abruptly. "I don't have time to put this nicely. You owe me. I need you. Simple. Clean."

That thought was appalling to her, the idea of working for him again. "There's nothing I can do that twenty other people under you couldn't do."

"I wouldn't be here if that was the case." His eyes were riveting, and she had no doubt that he knew everything that was going on in her mind. "I needed fast clearance, and you got it in twenty-four hours."

"How high is the clearance?"

"As high as I needed it to be. I want you to know that when this is over I'll consider us even."

He played his final card with the same tone of voice as the rest of the conversation, but she knew he knew she'd been waiting for it. "That's it?" she asked.

"That's it." He didn't wait for her agreement before he said, "Now let's get down to business."

Whitney held his gaze as long as she could, then finally closed her eyes and exhaled, knowing when she was backed into a corner. "Okay, what is it?"

"A man named Jacob Hill. I need you to get to him for me."

She looked back at him. "Why?"

He opened the briefcase, took out a single folder and tossed it onto the desk in front of her. "It's all in there. Background, the situation and everything you need on the man. I'll be calling you in the next twenty-four hours, and when I do, be ready to leave."

She didn't touch the briefcase. "Leave for where?"

"When I know that, I'll call. Then you'll know."

"My job here—"

"It's been taken care of."

"How do I get to see—"

He hit the briefcase with the flat of his hand, the sound as shattering as the thunder outside. "Details are my problem." Cutter had never shown any emotion other than a determination to do his job. Now his impatience was almost tangible. He obviously had a lot on the line, and he was pulling her into it with him. She could almost hate him for that.

"I didn't ask to be pulled into your problems," she said.

"None of us asked for this," he muttered, then exhaled and drew back. His control was in place in a split second. "Just know I'll take care of everything. I need you to take care of Jake Hill. Anything else?"

As she stared up at Cutter across the desk, she accepted the fact that any chance of her telling him to take his problem and get out was lost more than a year ago. She shook her head. "No."

"Stay close to the phone," he said as he picked up his briefcase and turned to head for the door.

"Cutter?"

He stopped as he pulled the door open and spoke without turning. "What?"

"When this is done, we're really even?"

"You've got my word on it," he said, then left, closing the door quietly behind him.

Whitney jumped when another bolt of lightning ripped through the heavens, followed by a rolling boom of thunder. Quickly she reached for the folder and looked at it. The name Jacob Michael Hill was written in bold black print across it and a security seal held it closed.

She tore the seal open and lifted the cover. Lying on top was a single four-by-six snapshot of a man, just head and shoulders. She picked it up and stared at an image that was both stark and riveting.

Deep brown eyes, as brooding as the night, dominated a gaunt face, with features etched by rough strokes into planes and angles. High cheekbones, a strong jaw and a wide mouth were emphasized by raven-black hair shot with gray, combed straight back from his face and worn long enough to lay on his shoulders.

She stared at the photo, taking in the mixture of repressed anger in the tightness that bracketed the mouth and a shadow of isolation in the narrowed eyes under straight dark brows. She'd seen that expression before, and it made her insides hurt. To see a man who was in danger of losing his humanity was a terrible thing.

Whitney laid the photo facedown on the desk, then she picked up the stack of papers in the file. As she sank back in her chair, she began to read about Jake Hill, and she wasn't surprised when she found out just what Cutter Ford wanted her to do.

Chapter 1

July 1

The call from Cutter came at noon the next day, and Whitney was on her way to the airport for a flight to Tucson, Arizona, less than an hour later. By four o'clock Arizona time, she was in a brand-new sports car, midnight black and sleek as an arrow, heading south on a two-lane highway to a tiny town called Bliss.

Cutter had spoken quickly on the phone, giving her a quick rundown on what she needed to know. "Pick up the car in the closest parking lot—no plates. Dealer signs—green, Hiller Motors. Keys will be under the front seat along with a map and a plastic box the size of a pack of cigarettes. When you spot the sign for Bliss, park on the shoulder and get out. Point the box at the car, press the button on the side, then get back in.

"The car will take you into Bliss before it breaks down. Hill's working at a place called Wally's Service Garage. The rest is up to you."

The car almost purred as she drove it, but she knew if Cutter said it would break down, it would. He always meant what he said. And he'd said her obligations to him were settled when she did this one job for him.

She glanced at the tote bag on the passenger seat, the bag she'd put the files in. Jacob Michael Hill, thirty-six, never married, engaged twice, a background of survival—from a childhood in foster homes, through the army where he'd been injured in a plane crash, to the corporate world, right up to a future that was a huge question mark. She'd read it all over and over again, finding out all she could about the target subject.

It made her a bit uncomfortable to be fitting back into the picture with Cutter so quickly. Study the subject, get all the background you can and figure out what questions to ask and how to ask them. Too quickly. It was as if there hadn't been a gap of months between her last job and this job.

She realized her hands were clenched on the steering wheel, and she eased her hold just as she spotted the sign for Bliss by the side of the road. Faded letters on sun-bleached wood proclaimed Bliss, Arizona, Gem Of The Valley, Pop. 2302.

As soon as she passed the sign, she slowed and pulled the car onto the shoulder, grimacing at the dust that billowed cloudlike behind her. In front of her was a small rise, and she couldn't see beyond it, but Bliss had to be a short distance ahead.

She turned off the car and reached for the plastic box. With it in hand, she got out into heat that was more oppressive than anything she'd felt before. Thankful for her sunglasses, she just wished she'd had time to change after Cutter's call. But she hadn't. So she'd traveled in her work clothes—navy linen slacks, a silk tailored long-sleeved shirt and low heels. The material was starting to stick to her skin already.

She stopped, held the plastic box out toward the car, pressed the button and heard a dull popping sound. But that was all. She waited for a moment, then cautiously got back in the car. Carefully she turned the key, but the engine started immediately. The air conditioner worked, making the dampness of her blouse chilly against her skin. For a moment she sat there, waiting for something else to happen.

Then a chime sounded and a digital readout just under the speedometer flashed on. Low Oil Pressure. It was starting. She quickly pulled back onto the deserted highway, and as she crested a low hill, off in the distance, she could barely make out Bliss baking in the setting sun. The town was little more than a shimmering, heat-distorted blur of low buildings that fanned out on either side of the highway, which ran right down its middle.

As she got closer and the buildings began to gain definition, she felt the car gradually begin to lose power. Another light flashed on the dash. Engine Hot. At the same time an acrid odor of something burning began to invade the interior of the car. With the town still a mile ahead, the engine began to clatter. Even though she pressed the accelerator more, the engine was losing power rapidly.

It wasn't going to make it to Bliss. As the thought formed, the car's engine died with a horrible clatter. She turned the key, but all that happened was a whining, cranking sound, clattering, then a low hiss. Steering toward the shoulder of the road, she managed to coast onto the rock and sand.

Whitney braked to a stop, then sank back in the seat and closed her eyes. She had at least a mile's walk in front of her because Cutter had been wrong. For what she thought was the first time since she met him, the man had miscalculated, but she was the one who was going to bake in the sun and try to walk in low heels.

But when she opened her eyes, she realized this wasn't Cutter's fault. She was the one who'd made a mistake. A metal road department sign for Bliss was about two hundred feet ahead of her, new and gleaming in the sun. She'd found the wrong sign, probably some old relic that people had forgotten about when the new sign was installed.

She looked at the setting sun and hoped that the station where Hill worked would be open when she finally got there.

Jake Hill had been drifting around the southwestern states for about three months, ever since he'd walked out on his job in Los Angeles and taken off on his motorcycle without looking back. Then three days ago he'd found Bliss, a town that was little more than a widening in the highway, a town long since passed by the interstate to the north. He'd arrived at sunset, got a job at the only service station and garage in town, and he'd stopped moving for a while. Until he had to again.

Maybe he'd stay longer here. He liked the heat and openness of the desert, the freedom of being able to take off from town in just about any direction and not see another human being for miles and miles. And for a while he might be able to forget. He might be able to believe that his life started three days ago, and that the past wasn't there to haunt him when he let down his guard. At least, he could let himself think that for a while, until it all started again.

Heading back to Bliss after going to see the location of an Indian burial ground in the low hills to the southeast, he rode his motorcycle down the blistering blacktop. The hot, dry air rushed past, touched with the pungency of exhaust and the burned fragrance of the desert.

Wally Lanier, his boss at the garage, had told Jake there were strange things that happened in the desert, mystical things that defied explanation. That's why the old man had told Jake to see the burial grounds. Ghosts walked the land, Wally had said, ghosts that were restless, ghosts that were looking for a place of peace.

Jake knew Wally was right. But the ghosts weren't Indians from the past. The ghosts came with Jake and they were all his. But since he'd been in Bliss, the ghosts had stayed at bay, and the nightmares hadn't started up again. But talk of ghosts and the memory of dreams made him uneasy.

As if he could outrun the past, he tugged his faded New York Yankees cap lower over his shoulder-length dark hair, then regripped the handles of the bike and turned up the throttle. The bike surged forward, and the valley slipped past. Rock formations soared to-

ward a sky streaked with the colors of twilight,
blurred, and the distant hills that rimmed the area cast
long shadows overland.

Not another human being was in sight, and Jake
could taste the freedom that emptiness gave him, until he crested a low rise in the road. Either he was seeing a mirage, something the spirits Wally talked about
had conjured up or a product of the unrelenting heat,
or someone was standing by the side of the road.

As he sped forward, he could make out a woman
with blond hair standing by a sleek black sports car.
She turned at the sound of his bike, then moved
quickly onto the pavement, waving her arms frantically for him to stop. Slowing, he could see she was a
slip of a thing, probably not more than an inch or two
over five feet.

She was dressed as if she was at some yuppie party
rather than standing in the desert in one hundred degree heat. Tailored dark slacks and a pale blouse clung
damply to her, emphasizing high breasts and the curve
of her slender hips.

She lowered her arms as he coasted to a stop on the
edge of the pavement just behind her car, then she
hurried toward him. Oversize sunglasses partially hid
her face, but he could see a slightly sharp chin, the elegant sweep of her throat and pale lips that smiled
with relief.

He balanced himself on the bike with his booted feet
planted on the baking pavement and slipped off his
sunglasses to swipe at the sweat on his face. Not more
than five feet from him, the woman's steps faltered.
For a moment he thought he saw shock in her expres-

sion, then it was gone as she made her way over the rough ground to where he sat on the idling bike.

He slipped his glasses back on as she called over the low rumble of the engine. "Thank you for stopping. I didn't think anyone would be out here at this time of day."

He glanced past her at the car. "What happened?"

"It just stopped. It's hot."

Jake hit the kickstand with his boot, then balanced the bike and swung off it, leaving it idling. As he turned to face the woman, he realized that at six feet he'd been right about her height. He was almost a foot taller than her. She tugged at the front of her blouse, trying to ease the material away from her skin, but all she succeeded in doing was emphasizing the fabric clinging to her breasts.

He looked away, the heat of the day enough for him right now. As he walked toward her car, he spoke to her over his shoulder. "How long did you drive it hot?"

He heard her hurrying after him. "Not very far."

He walked around to the front and touched the hood, but jerked back when he felt the fire in the metal. The car had overheated to the point that he wouldn't be surprised to find the spark plugs melted into the engine block. "Too far," he murmured. "Way too far."

He felt the woman beside him, her sleeve brushing his arm. "It just got hot and it smelled and it started clattering."

"It's too bad. It looks new." He glanced at her, the setting sun glinting off her glasses. "Is it this year's model?"

She shrugged, a fluttering movement of her shoulders that tugged the damp fabric of her blouse tighter across her breasts. "I guess so. I just didn't realize it was getting so hot."

For a moment Jake felt something he'd almost forgotten could happen to him. This woman was sexy, in the simplest sense of the word. Tiny and feminine, she struck a cord in him, and it seemed an eternity since he'd looked at any woman with anything more than a casual glance.

For no reason he found himself feeling a bit angry that a woman on the side of the road, a woman who didn't have a brain in her head when it came to cars, a woman who was a perfect stranger, could elicit anything from him on an emotional level.

"How in the hell couldn't you realize it? You've got gauges in that car that would make a jet look underregulated." He knew he was speaking harshly when he saw the way her smile died. Another emotion seemed to close around him. Regret. God knew he had regrets—monumental regrets—but it seemed forever since he'd regretted anything he said to a woman.

"I don't know much about cars," she said, swiping at the moisture-sleek skin of her throat and chin. "And I don't know a thing about this country out here. It's like a furnace."

Maybe Wally had been right, that the desert played with a man's mind out here. Or maybe he was finally going over the edge. Whatever was happening right now, whatever there was in this woman that made him feel so erratic emotionally, he stopped it with simple anger. Anger was a clean, neat emotion that could blot out anything else, so he embraced the anger he felt for her getting him into a situation that cut into his time alone. "Whatever happened, it's going to cost you a fortune to fix it . . . *if* it can be fixed."

She fanned her hand in front of her face in an attempt to stir the hot air. "I don't care what it costs— all I want is to get out of this heat and find a garage so I can get it towed."

"There you're in luck. There's a garage in Bliss with a towing rig. I'm heading there, so I'll let them know you're out here." He turned to walk away, to get back to his bike and take off, but she stopped him in his tracks by grasping his forearm.

The contact startled him, and he acted before he thought, jerking his arm free. He hated being touched. It made him feel . . . no word came to him. But he knew the last person he wanted to touch him right now was this woman.

"You aren't going to leave me out here, are you?" she asked as she drew her hand back.

Getting involved was something he just didn't do anymore, and getting help for her was the extent of involvement he could offer. "Someone'll be here in fifteen minutes. Just go back to your car—"

"No, I'll go to the garage with you." She hurried to the driver's side of the car, opened the door and leaned inside. When she moved back and slammed the door, she had a wallet in her hand. Without a word, she started for his bike.

He hurried after her, easily getting to the bike at the same time she did. "Listen, lady, I've only got this motorcycle and it's no taxi."

"It's fine," she said as she swiped at moisture on her cheek. "I'm really not particular right now."

He shook his head. "If we crash, you're going to lose every inch of skin under those fancy clothes."

She squared to face him, her chin lifting just a bit. "You aren't exactly in protective clothes yourself," she said, pointing out the obvious about his jeans and T-shirt.

"I don't have a helmet for you, either."

"And you aren't wearing a helmet."

"Whatever chances I take with myself are my business, but you—"

"I can take whatever chances I want to take with myself." She blew her breath upward, stirring her pale hair at her forehead. "Besides, I'd rather move in this heat than sit and bake in a car. A hot breeze is better than no breeze."

Jake gave up. He wasn't going to stand here and argue with her. "Do what you want," he said and threw his leg over the bike to settle in the seat.

Before he knew what was happening, the woman grabbed him again, but this time she was using him for leverage to get on the back of the bike. He closed his eyes tightly as she maneuvered into position. When she settled against his back, one hand at his waist, he cast her a glance over his shoulder.

His hate of touching was magnified every time she made contact, and he had done all he could do not to yell at her to let him go. "If you're going to insist on doing this," he advised, "hold on to the sides of the seat, not to me, and keep your feet on the sidebar and away from the exhaust pipes."

She shifted the way he'd told her to do, then she said, "Do you have someplace to put my wallet? I can't hold on to the seat and hold it, too."

He reached back over his shoulder, and she put it into his hand. The fine leather felt warm from her grip, and he quickly pushed it under the front of his seat to secure it.

She settled, a bit of space between her body and his, and he almost felt relief at the contact being broken. But any relief was short-lived when her knees pressed against the outside of his thighs. He didn't know which contact was more unsettling, body to body, or her leg to his thigh.

He muttered an oath that was drowned out by the roar of the engine as he revved it. With a squeal of tires on the pavement, he took off in the direction of Bliss.

Whitney didn't know what surprised her more, to find that Jacob Michael Hill was sitting in front of her on a black-and-chrome motorcycle in jeans, a T-shirt and worn cowboy boots, or to find out that the picture Cutter had given her didn't come anywhere close to the reality.

Nothing had prepared her for a man who was whipcord lean, with tanned skin, sinewy arms, long hair touched with gray partially hidden by a well-worn baseball cap, and a tangible aura of nervous impatience to get out of her proximity.

She held tightly to the seat of the motorcycle as the sounds of the roaring engine and rushing air filled the space around her. But she never took her eyes off Jake, nor could she ignore where her knees pressed against the rough denim that encased his muscular thighs. She felt the tension in him, the constant need to keep his balance as he drove the big machine and his uneasiness at her being on the bike with him.

His hair tangled in the wind, occasionally brushing across her face, and his shoulders strained under the cotton of the plain T-shirt. Damp patches clung to his shoulders and back, and a deep tan on his arms was stark against the white material. Cutter hadn't said anything about a motorcycle, but it fit the pattern she'd built for the man from the files.

No restrictions, no bonds. She bet he slept outside most of the time, too. And she knew that Cutter had actually been wise in sending her here with a cover story. If Jake Hill knew what she was after, he'd put her off the bike, and he'd drive into the sunset, leaving her to the heat, the desert and the buzzards. He'd been close to doing that just a moment ago without having any concept of who he'd rescued.

She narrowed her eyes behind her sunglasses and caught a glimpse of Bliss over Jake's shoulder. The town was tiny, just the way she thought it would be, with a main street of small business interspersed with old houses. The town was old, with false fronts on some of the businesses, wooden sidewalks raised six inches above the line of the road and hitching rails here and there.

She caught glimpses of the side streets as they passed on the bike, most of them unpaved with towering trees on the sides that cast long shadows. Few people were out and around in the late afternoon, and just a car or two slowly cruised by. A bright red-white-and-blue banner hung across the main intersection in town, a slack piece of material splashed with stars and stripes, announcing July Fourth, Founder's Day Rodeo And Carnival.

As they coasted through the intersection, she spotted Wally's Service Garage. Jake swung the bike into the gravel parking area and glided to a stop by the open doors of the service bay. Thankfully it was in the shade of the wood-fronted building. Even though the sun was almost behind the hills, any shade was welcome in the heat.

With the motorcycle idling at a low rumble, Jake turned and spoke over his shoulder. "We're here," he said.

Whitney scrambled off the bike and steadied herself with one hand pressed flat to the rough wooden wall of the garage. She'd never been on a motorcycle in her life, and she hadn't known that her legs would still be shaking even without the massive bike under her.

She turned to Jake and realized she hated dark glasses. All she could see was her own face reflected back in the lenses, a face framed by mussed hair and partially hidden by her own glasses. She just wished she could see Jake's eyes. "Wally!" he called out.

Whitney glanced at the garage door when a bear of man in greasy coveralls ambled out of the dimness. Barrel chested, wearing a dark Stetson over salt-and-pepper hair and with a well-lined face dominated by a large nose, the man was wiping his soiled hands on a rag. "Jake? What's going on?"

"Wally, this lady's got car trouble."

The owner of the garage. Whitney smiled at him. "I *do* have car trouble."

Wally shook his head from side to side as hazel eyes under a grizzled brow studied her. "Send this guy up into the hills to commune with the spirits and look what he brings back. A beautiful lady."

"He found me with a dead car about a mile out of town, and he was nice enough to give me a ride here so I could get the car towed and maybe get it fixed."

"You're in luck, little lady. I'm Wally Lanier and I've got the only tow truck for fifty miles around."

"Then I'm in the right place." Wally glanced at Jake, his smile gone. "What's the problem with her car?"

"It boiled over."

"Is it vapor locked, or—"

"It's fried," Jake confirmed.

The old man looked back at Whitney. "How long did you drive it hot?"

"I don't know. The warning light flashed on, then the car just sort of clattered and died."

He wiped at his hands one last time with the rag, then tossed it over his shoulder and it landed on the hood of a car on the lift in the garage. "I'll tell you what, I can go tow it now so it won't sit out all night, and I might have time to look at before I close down. But as far as fixing it, that's something else again." He tugged his black hat a bit lower. "It might take till tomorrow or the next day before I can tell you what the damage is, or if I can fix it. And we're looking at a holiday thrown in."

"That's fine. I'm on vacation, so I've got the time. As long as you've got a hotel close by?"

"We've got one hotel, and that's about it."

"How close is it?"

"Half a mile straight down Main Street this side of the town limits." He looked at Jake. "You're going there, aren't you, Jake?"

"I was planning on it, but since you're towing—"

"I can take care of the tow. How about taking the little lady there, then come on back here, and get Gibson's car done? By then I'll be back and we can check out her car together."

Jake hesitated, and before he could refuse to do it Whitney spoke up. "I would really appreciate a ride. This heat is a killer, and I'm not used to it at all."

He glanced at her, the setting sun glinting off the metal frames of his sunglasses. Then he shrugged. "Get on."

Wally held out his hand. "I'll need the key."

She'd completely forgotten to take the key with her. "It's in the ignition."

"Okay, and what name do I put on your bill?"

"Whitney Tate."

"Where're you from, Miss Tate?"

"Back east." She got back on the bike behind Jake, being careful not to touch him this time. Before he could tell her to, she gripped the seat and tucked her feet on the bar away from the exhaust.

"Tell Emma at the hotel that I sent you and I'm working on your car," Wally said as he stood back from the bike. "She'll give you a break on the price."

"Thanks," she called over the burst of noise as Jake revved the engine.

Wally touched his Stetson, then Jake swung to the left and back to the street. He turned in the opposite direction of the way they'd just come, and when they were just past the last side street, he slowed and swung right. He drove onto a driveway lined with a low-growing ground cover that splashed brilliant reds and pinks alongside the dull brown-and-gray gravel.

At the top of the curve in the driveway sat the hotel, a sprawling adobe-and-wood building with a weathered tile roof protected by ancient olive and eucalyptus trees. Pots of geraniums decorated a front porch that ran the length of the structure, and soft light spilled out into the gathering dusk of evening from a series of arched windows. The porch held a few small tables, and by the double front doors an old-fashioned swing slowly moved back and forth, but no one was in sight.

Jake stopped by the shallow porch steps, then glanced back at Whitney. "The Bliss Hotel."

She got off, knowing he would be gone in a moment, and she tried to prolong the contact. "Who did Wally say to talk to?"

"Emma, his wife." As he slipped off his sunglasses and tucked them in the pocket on his T-shirt, she had her wish. She was looking into deep brown eyes narrowed by thick, dark lashes. But they gave away nothing. "They own this place."

"And I thought he was sending me here so he'd get a kickback from the owner," she joked.

The attempted humor fell flat as Jake shrugged. "Sure," he said, then revved the bike and took off down the driveway. He drove out onto the street and headed back in the direction of the station without looking back.

"Thanks for the ride," Whitney murmured to the emptiness around her as the noise from the motorcycle died out. She'd known it wouldn't be easy to talk with Jake Hill, but she'd never run into such a solid cement wall before. If she got what Cutter wanted, it would more than make them even.

Chapter 2

Whitney turned and went up the steps of the hotel,
across the wood plank porch and reached for the entry door. She pulled it back and stepped into the lobby,
a space that stretched from the front of the hotel to the
back. Through a wall of wood-trimmed glass doors at
the back, she could see a sprawling courtyard. The
shadows of trees outside were softened by tiny twinkling lights in the foliage that made it look like a million fireflies.

  She looked around at the mixture of Spanish and
western antiques. Worn clay tiles in the lobby area
seemed to emanate coolness and complemented the
dark wood reception desk to the right and the brass
pots against the white plaster walls. Plush beige car-
pet on the back part of the space marked a small restaurant area with several tables draped in white linen

with a single candle in the middle of each, set for the view out the back doors.

A heavy-beamed ceiling supported two huge fans that slowly stirred the air, and three low chandeliers with brass shades cast a soft glow over the area. There wasn't a soul in sight, and when Whitney spotted a pay phone near a display case filled with jewelry and souvenirs set up by the reception desk, she crossed to it.

Quickly she put in a collect call to Cutter's office in Washington.

As the operator put the call through, Whitney said, "Cutter? I'm here."

"Where's here?"

"Bliss, Arizona." She looked around the room. "I'm staying at the Bliss Hotel. It's the only one in town, so you can get the number if you need it."

"Have you contacted Hill?"

"He found me stranded by the side of the road after the car gave out."

"What a break for us."

"He's staying at this hotel, too."

"Very good work."

Any praise from Cutter made Whitney uncomfortable. She wasn't here to win his praise, just to win a final end to her time working for him. "What exactly did you do to the car?"

"Just cracked the drain plug for the oil. Cars can't run without oil."

She had a feeling that Jake Hill wouldn't be fooled too easily. "Will anyone be able to tell it was done on purpose?"

"No. It'll look like a failure in the part, or that you maybe hit a rock or something and broke it. If you're asked, say you got off the road for a bit. Don't worry about that. The car's expendable.''

"What about Jake Hill?" she found herself asking.

"We're working for the greater good on this job," Cutter said in his usual even tone. "We do what we have to do."

"And what if getting what we need from Hill damages him?"

"I'll regret that, *if* it happens. We've offered him help, and he refused. He left his job and disappeared. We were damned lucky to find him at all. Now I think he can help us, and you're there to find out if I'm right. Just do what I asked you to do, and we'll take care of the fallout later."

That was probably how Cutter saw Bob Fillerman's suicide. Fallout. Something that couldn't be anticipated or avoided. The man just went over the edge after what he'd been through. But she had never been capable of seeing a life as expendable, and that's exactly why she'd changed jobs and hadn't been involved in anything like this for more than a year.

"I'm no psychiatrist. But I've seen enough people go through hell, then come back to their normal life without a prayer of being able to do it on their own. Those people are like walking time bombs, unless someone helps defuse them." She couldn't forget the closed look in Jake's eyes. "Jake Hill needs help, Cutter."

"I told you, he was offered all kinds of help, believe me. But no one can force him into therapy."

"You should have insisted."

"This is still a free country. Let's keep it that way."

"I didn't have a choice about what I'm doing."

Cutter exhaled harshly over the line. "Whitney, just don't try to analyze what you're doing, or even justify it. Just do it. It's the end results that count."

"And Jake Hill is a means to an end."

"Right now he is."

Whitney knew that Cutter's ability to categorize and stay emotionally uninvolved made him good at what he did. Any man who could deal with the kind of people he did—terrorists and crazies—and make sense out of it all, even save lives, put him a world away from what she could endure. "I often wonder if you ever see people as people, Cutter?"

"Of course I do. That's why I do what I do. If I didn't, I wouldn't be in the job I'm in. No one can get caught in a life-and-death situation without putting a value on human life."

"How do you choose which life has more value?"

"I don't. I get an assignment and do it. That's the bottom line. I've got a job and you're helping me. I need you to find out if Hill holds the key to the information we need in his memory."

But memories could kill a man like Jake Hill. She knew that all too well. "That sounds so neat and clean."

"Nothing's neat and clean in this life, or I'd be out of work." She knew that was just about as philosophical as Cutter Ford ever got. "Let me know when you know anything."

"Where are you going to be over the holiday weekend?"

"Right here at the office."

Whitney realized that she had never known much about Cutter's private life. Or even if he had one. Despite an expensive apartment in Georgetown, he seemed to live at his office. "I'll be in touch," she said.

The moment she hung up she sensed that someone was right behind her, waiting and listening. She turned, not sure what she expected, but it was Jake standing there, not more than three feet from her. She hadn't heard a thing.

His glasses were still off, his dark hair tucked behind his ears and the brim of his hat pulled low, partially shading his face. She didn't have any idea what he'd heard or what he hadn't, because his expression was closed, controlled and painfully unreadable. This man totally disproved the old notion that the eyes were the windows to the soul. She knew that it was impossible for a human being to exist without a soul, but some were tortured, some weren't and some just existed.

"I didn't hear you come in," she said.

"I thought you would have heard the bike."

She had been so tangled up in her conversation with Cutter that she hadn't. Now his voice, without the constant throbbing of the motorcycle engine in the background, was deep and rough and low. It fit him someway. "I'm sorry. I was on the phone."

"I got to the station before I found this." He held out her wallet to her. "I thought you might need it."

She looked at her wallet, the thought that there might be something in it to link her to Cutter coming to her in a flash. Jake's expression was so unreadable. Quickly she took the wallet and opened it. "I forgot about it."

"I didn't go through it," Jake said.

She looked back at him, his eyes narrowed under his dark eyebrows. "Oh, I wasn't thinking—"

"Why not? You don't know me."

She tugged at the blouse that clung uncomfortably to her skin, and she wished she could get out into lighter, fresh clothes. "I appreciate you bringing it back. I was wondering, my luggage is in the car and—"

He cut her off again. "As soon as the car's at the garage, we'll send it over for you."

"Well, I thought I heard people out here talking," someone said to Whitney's left.

Whitney glanced and saw an older woman coming out of swinging doors by the reception desk. Dressed in jeans and a plain blouse under a long, soiled apron, the woman had pulled back her reddish hair into a ponytail. She held her hands up in front of her, much like a surgeon would have after scrubbing before an operation as she smiled at Whitney. "So you're the woman Wally sent over?"

"Yes, I am."

"Wally's gone to tow her car," Jake said. "I have to get back."

He was at the door before Whitney could turn, then she watched him step out into the evening, and the door closed behind him.

"He's an odd one, isn't he?"

Whitney looked back at the woman who now stood right behind the desk as she peeled off the yellow gloves. "Odd?" Whitney asked. Maybe this lady would be able to fill in some blanks about Jake for her. "How so?"

The woman smiled dismissively as she dropped her gloves on the desk. "You know the kind—now you see him, now you don't. He just showed up at Wally's three days ago looking for work. God knows how long he'll stick around."

Whitney went closer to the desk. "You don't know him very well?"

"No, but I've seen the type. He's running. Wally asked him if he was in trouble with the police, but he said he wasn't." She reached under the desk and took out an old-fashioned guest book, laid it on the scarred wooden counter and opened it. As she spun it around for Whitney, she said, "Just sign in, and we'll fix you up."

Whitney reached for a pen from a holder to her right, then looked at the registration page. The last guest was J. Hill, home address left empty, length of stay left empty. The guest above him had signed in almost a month ago. As she wrote her name and her Virginia address, she said, "It doesn't look like you have much of a turnover in guests."

"We used to be full all the time, then they built the interstate and those days were gone. Not that I'm too sad about it. Now I've got time to do things I couldn't before."

When Whitney put the pen back, the woman turned the ledger and read, "Whitney Tate." Gray eyes met hers and the woman smiled. "I'm Emma, owner and manager of this place."

And a wealth of any information she might have managed to glean, Whitney thought. "I saw the sign for the rodeo and carnival. I would have thought you'd be pretty full by now."

Emma shook her head. "No. Lots of people come, but mostly for the day. And the rest that go are local folks. We're real big on patriotic holidays, even in the heat of summer." She closed the ledger. "Any preference on rooms? Front or back, with a patio or not? The hotel is laid out like a giant U-shape, with private patios for the back rooms." She pointed to the back doors. "There's the main courtyard for guests to use. Although right now there's just you and Jake staying here."

"Where's he from?"

"No idea. He never said. In fact, he just moved in here last night. The other two nights he camped out behind Wally's station. Wally talked him into getting a room. Never know when a friendly snake will sidle up to you and make you regret sleeping on the ground."

The woman was a talker, and Whitney was going to encourage that. "I guess a hotel is definitely better than that."

"Yeah." She closed the book. "So what kind of room do you want? You've got your pick of the place."

"If you've only got one other guest, why not give me the room next to his?"

"Boy, you're easy. Jake was real particular. Had to be a back room, a corner room, and when he looked at what was available he took the one that's got a wall of doors that open so it's like the wall almost disappears. Thing is, he's left the doors open ever since he moved in. If he's using the air conditioner, it's going to be eating up our electric.''

Whitney listened to Emma talking about Jake as a guest, but heard the description of a man on the edge. He wasn't able to cope, carrying a burden that weighed him down tremendously and made walls or any type of confinement anathema to him.

''Some people don't like closed spaces,'' she said.

''Maybe he's got problems, too.'' Emma grabbed a key out of an old-fashioned pigeonhole letter sorter behind her, then came out from behind the desk. ''All right, let me show you the room next to Jake's, and you can tell me if it's to your liking.''

Whitney followed Emma across the lobby through an archway into a wide hall. They went almost to a curve in the corridor, then stopped by a door on the right marked 5A. Emma slipped a key in the lock and glanced at Whitney. ''I could put you on the other end and give you lots of privacy.''

Whitney looked at the next door, 7A, and shook her head. ''No this will be just fine.''

Jake didn't head back to the hotel until just before eleven o'clock that night. After he'd sent the lady's luggage to the hotel, he and Wally had torn apart Whitney Tate's expensive sports car. And it was a mess. Even before they pulled the engine tomorrow, it was obvious it was going to cost a fortune to fix the damage the oil loss had done.

He rode his motorcycle up to the front of the hotel and stopped by the old stone hitching post just past the steps. When he turned off the engine, the night surrounded him with the chorus of insects, night birds and the sweetness of blossoms on the balmy air. Twinkling lights ran along the top of the porch, and the hotel sign in the lawn by the curve in the driveway was softly lit.

Jake got off his bike and headed for the stairs, taking them in one long stride. The porch squeaked under his weight as he stepped onto the planks, then a soft, husky voice came out of the shadows to his left.

"Any news on the patient?"

He turned and could barely make out someone sitting on the swing in the shadows. The feeling of being watched made him uneasy.

"My car," Whitney Tate said, her voice blending into the softness of the desert night, yet skimming uneasily over his nerves. "The one I fried this afternoon. Remember?"

He stayed where he was, trying to see her in the shadows. "It's dead."

"What caused it to break down?"

"You broke the oil drain plug, cracked the oil pan, lost your oil and basically ran the car without oil."

As they spoke, his eyes gradually adjusted to the dimness until he could see her curled up in the corner of the wooden porch swing. She had one arm resting on the back, one leg tucked under her, the other making lazy circles over the plank floor. She was staring right at him.

"That sounds really bad," she said in a muted tone.

He caught the suggestion of sweet blossoms in the night air. "Just about as bad as it gets."

"What's Wally going to do?"

"Probably tell you to contact the dealer and find out what they'll do for you under your warranty."

"Can't he fix it here?"

"I suppose if he had to he could, but—"

"Then fix it." She stood and silently came over to him. It was then he realized that the gentle fragrance of blossoms clung to her, a combination of the night and heat and softness. "Just tell him to fix it," she repeated as she looked up at him.

She'd changed into fresh clothes, a dark tank top and very short white shorts that exposed slender arms and long legs. A trick of the dim light made her pale hair look as if it glowed around her upturned face. "Fix it? Just like that?" he asked.

"I can pay whatever it takes."

"Good for you," he said with a touch of sarcasm he hadn't really intended.

She didn't act as if he'd offended her. "It doesn't hurt to have a bit of money at times like these."

"Well, whatever you do, you'll have to talk to Wally about it. He's the boss. He'll be back here in half an hour or so." He started to turn and go inside, but she stopped him.

"Jake?"

The use of his first name carried a shade of intimacy with it, and it disturbed him vaguely to hear her say it on the warm softness of night. He glanced back at her. "What?"

"Thanks for sending my luggage over. It was a relief to get into cooler clothes." She held out her hand to him. "And thanks again for all your help today. I had visions of dying in the desert in linen slacks and a long-sleeved blouse, with buzzards circling overhead."

He ignored her hand, the memory of her behind him on the bike too vivid right then to make contact with her. "You weren't in any danger of dying," he murmured, keeping his hands at his sides.

She drew back. "Why don't you sit out here for a while with me and have some lemonade?"

"I don't want any," he said.

"Won't you change your mind? Emma makes the best lemonade I've ever tasted."

Either she didn't get the point that he was trying to make his escape, or she was just plain stubborn. "Thanks, but it's been a long day."

"Are you sure?"

If he needed anything right then, it was a good stiff drink, something to take his mind off a sudden thought of touching her, holding her, kissing her and using her to push back the loneliness of the night. That last thought jarred him. Using her? That's exactly what he would be doing with any woman he was with now.

"I'm calling it a night," he said and turned from her to go to the door.

"Thanks again," she called after him. "Maybe another time."

Jake stepped into the hotel lobby, letting the door shut behind him with a thud, but even when he got to his room and closed the door, he could almost hear Whitney saying, "Maybe another time." He knew that would never be.

The patio doors were all open, and the heat of the day had invaded the room. A small price to pay to feel as if he could breathe. In the silence of the spacious room, he stripped off his clothes, and when he stepped under the coolness of the shower, he did his best to forget about the woman in the shadows on the porch.

Whitney didn't wait for Wally to come back to the hotel. Ten minutes after Jake went inside, she went inside. As she went down the hallway to her room, she tried to figure out what she was going to do the next day. First of all, she had to be around Jake as much as possible. That meant getting up early, going to the service station and staying there all day if she had to.

She went into her room where the soft purr of the wall air conditioner and the slowly swooshing sound from the rotating overhead fan were the only sounds she heard. She slipped off her sandals, and the tile floor in the large room felt cool under her feet. The off-white walls and the bleached-wood furniture, made the room feel light and comfortable.

When she undressed and slipped on an oversize T-shirt to sleep in, she tugged back the dusty-rose spread on the poster bed and climbed in between the cool linen sheets. For what seemed a very long time, she stared at the night through the glass doors. The dark shadows of huge trees in the courtyard was softened by the twinkling lights draped in them, making them look almost like something out of a fairy tale.

But there was nothing fairy-tale-like about the life Jake Hill led. He was a man in pain, a man hiding from part of his life, and a man who was closed and shuttered. She'd never felt completely assured that she knew what to ask a person like Jake, but being trained in debriefing, she knew that the right combination of words could make the darkness inside a person spill out.

That's what Cutter expected her to do, to get Jake to tell her about the dark recesses of his memory. But she wasn't at all sure she had the ability to do it with him. And if she did, if she managed to get Jake to remember his past in detail, she wasn't at all sure she was capable of dealing with the fallout. She rolled onto her side and pulled her legs up to her stomach. Closing her eyes tightly, she concentrated on falling asleep.

Darkness all around. A stench so potent that it burned his nose and throat. The terror was everywhere, and the silence was so tangible that he knew all he had to do was reach out, grab it and tear it into shreds. But he couldn't close his hands, the swelling making it impossible to bend his fingers. And he couldn't scream anymore, his throat was raw and swollen. The silence beat on his ears.

He huddled in the corner of his prison, "the hole," his back against the rough wooden wall and his heels dug into the damp dirt floor. He was suffocating from the stench and the heat. Then the gun was at his head, and the trigger pulled again and again until he begged for it to stop.

The laughter came, a high, shrill, ugly sound, and his tormentor struck out with a blow to Jake's head, then to his middle. Stinging pain ripped at his back, and his screams came out as indistinguishable groans.

"Help me," he begged in his mind, "help me," but there was no help, no one to push away the horror. And the voice of his tormentor was in his ear. "To-morrow. You die tomorrow."

Jake woke violently, sitting bolt upright. He was on the floor by the doors of his room, the bedroll he'd used as a cushion gone and the cold, hard tiles under his body.

His breathing was tight and rapid, his body soaked with sweat, and all he knew was he wanted to escape. He scrambled to his feet, reached for his jeans and boots and put them on. Without bothering to get his T-shirt, he went through the doors into the night.

When Whitney heard something outside, she glanced at the bedside clock and she saw it was midnight. Her internal clock hadn't caught up with the time difference from Washington D. C. to here, and she'd been lying wide-awake in bed since she first lay down.

She threw back the sheets and padded barefoot to the closed patio doors to look out. Someone was walking in the shadows on the edge of the main courtyard, then as the person stepped into the pale light of a partial moon she recognized Jake.

She didn't give herself time to think about it, but took the opportunity for any contact at all. Quickly slipping on her short pink cotton robe, she didn't bother with slippers. She quietly opened the patio doors and stepped out into the night. The worn cobbles on the patio felt smooth and warm under her bare feet. A gentle night breeze skimmed warm air over her face and bare legs as she crossed the tiny patio to the low brick wall that separated it from the main courtyard.

She went through the opening in the wall and hurried into the courtyard, heading for an ancient olive tree in the center of the area. She spotted Jake by a wrought-iron fence at the back of the hotel grounds, but before she could go after him, he'd opened a gate in the fence and gone through.

Beyond the fence, she could see a vast flat area spotted by the silhouettes of cactus, scrub brush and runted trees. Far off in the distance, she could see ridges of sculpted land, hulking shadows towering skyward.

With her bare feet she couldn't follow Jake, and if she went back inside to get her shoes, he'd be gone before she could come back out again. She didn't want to take that chance. Sooner or later he would come back, so she'd wait for him.

She crossed to one of the park benches that ringed the central area, sat down on the warm wooden seat and watched Jake go off into the distance. Gradually his image became a blur, then he was gone, blending into the shadows and the night.

Jake walked into the desert until he couldn't go any farther. When he finally stopped, he felt as if ghosts were at his back, that if he turned quickly he could see them.

He stared straight ahead, fighting the memory of the horrors that came out of the darkness in his soul when he least expected it. It had been awhile since he'd remembered any of the past, and for it to come now wrenched him. Someway he'd thought that here in Bliss maybe he could forget, that the memories would stay hidden, out of sight, out of mind, and he could feel halfway normal for a while.

But he couldn't. He was lost in that darkness, so deep in it that it almost seemed more real than life itself. Pain tore through him. As the night surrounded him, he threw back his head, thrust his arms heavenward and screamed, the sound like nothing human. It cut through the desert, ringing back at him from the distant hills. Yet even as it died out, he knew the horrors that lurked in dark places in his mind hadn't been scared away.

Nothing could do that.

He looked at the ridges far ahead of him that rose stark and rugged into the night sky. Maybe if he climbed to the top of the highest one, he would be able to hide from the horrors.

He knew the answer even before the question fully formed in his mind. He'd never be able to do that. He never had. He never would. If he got to the top of the world, the only thing that would stop the torment was to cease to exist. Then the memories would be well and truly dead.

He sank to his knees on the dusty ground, his head bowed. He stayed there, alone in the night, until he lost the urge to keep going and find the top of the world. Then slowly he got to his feet, pushed his hands in the pockets of his jeans and headed back to the hotel.

Chapter 3

The squeaking of the wrought-iron gate at the back of the courtyard startled Whitney, and she realized she'd fallen into a light sleep. Without any idea how long she'd been waiting on the bench, she sat straight and looked up to see Jake closing the gate. When he turned and started toward the hotel, he moved slowly, and she could almost feel his reluctance in returning.

She stood, then moved toward the center of the courtyard just as Jake reached the same area. "Hello," she said. Jake stopped immediately and turned in her direction. He was shirtless, wearing only jeans and boots. His hair fell loose from a center part to his shoulders. His face was shadowed, but even in the dimness she could see the tension in his expression. "I thought I was alone out here," she said.

"So did I," he murmured.

"I couldn't sleep. How about you?"

He raked his fingers through his hair, combing it back to expose his face, then he exhaled harshly. "I was walking."

"There's lots of empty spaces around here." She could tell he wanted to get away, just the way he had on the porch earlier. But she wasn't going to let him go that easily this time. "Sometimes, when I can't sleep, talking helps."

He stared at her, not saying a thing.

"I mean, just sitting and relaxing and talking," she said quickly. "Sometimes it helps the nightmares."

She knew as soon as she said it, she shouldn't have used the word "nightmares." He hadn't said a thing about having nightmares, but she would have bet all she had that they were what had driven him from the hotel earlier.

"What are you talking about?"

She shrugged, trying to regroup. "I mean, if a person can't sleep, for whatever reason, it sometimes helps to talk to someone else."

"What are you, a therapist of some sort?"

"No."

"A psychiatrist, maybe?"

"No."

"Then just what are you, Miss Tate?"

"Someone who's trying to make conversation."

"That's your mistake."

"What?"

"You don't have to *try* to do anything. Nothing's required. This isn't teatime, or some organized recreational activity. It's a chance meeting in the middle of the night at a hotel that has only two guests."

Boy, had she gone about this all wrong. She was used to offices and organized questions, not ad-libbing in the middle of the night and misreading the situation so completely. The man just wanted to be alone. Period. And he wasn't about to welcome the chance to have a midnight talk. "I'm sorry. I thought pleasantries were a mark of a civilized society."

He was silent for a long, strained moment, then shook his head. "I guess I'm not very civilized," he muttered.

"Maybe you're just out of practice."

"Maybe I was civilized at one time, but chose not to be now."

"I guess it doesn't matter as long as you know what you're doing with my car."

She expected him to say something cutting or to just turn and walk away. But she didn't expect a low, rough sound from him that could have been the hint of laughter. "So Whitney Tate's a woman who can obviously get to the bottom line when she has to."

"I guess so, *and* she knows when to say goodnight."

He nodded. "Good." Then he started across the worn tiles toward his room.

When Whitney fell in step beside him, he stopped on the edge of the courtyard and cast her a narrowed look. "I thought you said good-night?"

"I did. I'm going to my room. It's right next door to yours."

In the pale light from the moon overhead she saw a frown tug at his features. She hated the idea that the laughter was completely gone. "I guess there's no law against that," he murmured and walked away from her.

When they got near their rooms, Jake stopped and glanced at Whitney. "Miss Tate—"

"Whitney. My name's Whitney."

"It's not easy for me to make small talk. I'm not good at it anymore."

Whitney suddenly felt regret that she had never met the man Jake Hill had been before his ordeal. This man he had become was so closed it was painful to be with him in a one-on-one situation. But she didn't have a choice about being here, so she made herself say words that she knew were going to stir him—one way or another. "I think it's an unwritten rule that life isn't supposed to be easy."

She could see him react by narrowing his eyes as if he didn't want to see anything outside of himself. And her impulse to make it better, to cut off the impact of what she'd said, was overwhelming. Impulsively she reached out and touched him on the arm. But that only made things worse.

He jerked from the contact as if she'd burned him, and he bit out, "Life's a bitch."

His words hit a nerve in her that she could have sworn had healed. But it hadn't. The last one to say that to her had been Bob Fillerman—three hours before he threw himself from the tenth-floor window at his hotel.

The thought of a world without Jake Hill produced a pain she could barely absorb. Her hand clenched, the feel of him still lingering on her skin. "It doesn't have to be, Jake. I swear, it doesn't have to be."

He looked down at her, then unexpectedly he reached out as if to touch her cheek, but made no contact. His fingers hovered so close to her skin that she could feel his body heat. "I'm sick of lies," he muttered. "Lies and empty platitudes. Life isn't worth the effort."

"I'm not lying," she whispered. "I swear I'm not."

When this woman with huge moon-shadowed eyes and a halo of spun-gold hair told him that a life he had barely endured for what seemed an eternity could be different, anger grew in Jake. He touched her face with the tips of his fingers, the shock of the contact ricocheting through him. Contact was the last thing he wanted, yet as if driven by a force outside of him his hand cupped her chin.

"You don't know what my life's been," he growled.

Her tongue darted out to touch her pale lips. "I know it can hurt, Jake, that it can be almost unbearable."

Was she psychic? Was she some sort of witch that was weaving a spell around him? Or had he just been so long without a woman that anything she said would seem as if she could see into his soul? The night had been long and distorted, and his next impulse was even more off balance.

Hormones or need? He had no answers, but the next thing he knew he moved toward Whitney and found her lips with his. If he had been shaky before, the kiss threw him totally out of control. A bolt of lightning couldn't have demanded his attention more completely, or startled and frightened him more.

Yet the cause was so simple—an alien sweetness that seemed to be everywhere, her silky cheek under his hand, her lips parted softly in surprise. Everything was falling apart and as terrifying to him as the dreams that had driven him from the hotel earlier. Most terrifying to him was a sudden, inexplicable need for this woman, something that went beyond lust, yet centered on an urgency to take her here and now. Her touch on him earlier had felt like fire, but now his total being was in danger of being consumed.

Raw fear drove him to move back—fear as primitive as anything he had ever known, even in "the hole." He shoved his hands behind his back and, with one look at her face bathed in moonlight, the fear grew.

God help him, if he let himself go he could lose himself completely in her. He could just cease to be. His fingernails dug into the palms of his hands, and he tried to draw air into his tight lungs. She stared up at him, the shock inside him a mere hint in her expression.

"Why did you—"

He cut her off as the question formed because he had no answers, not even for himself. "Sorry," he muttered. There were no more words to say. Nothing. The emptiness was an ache inside him, and he turned from her. He walked away, through the opening in his patio wall and to the doors of his room.

Only when he touched the door frame did he chance a look back. But the night was empty. Whitney Tate was gone as surely as if she had been a ghost he'd conjured up. He turned and went inside. Sleep was impossible, and he couldn't take another dream. He scooped up his shirt, tugged it over his head and quietly crossed to the hall door and slipped out. In a matter of seconds he was going out the front door, and leaving his bike parked by the hitching post, he walked off down the driveway.

Whitney woke from a restless sleep as the light of dawn began to creep into her room through the glass windows of the doors. She pushed away the sheets tangled around her legs and felt the chill from leaving the air conditioner on high last night after she'd come in from her encounter with Jake.

She sat up slowly, then put her legs over the side of the bed as those moments with Jake came back to her with clarity. She had had no idea he was going to kiss her, not after the way he'd acted whenever he was touched. He hated that skin-to-skin contact, and she'd bet that he avoided it whenever he could.

Not only didn't she understand his actions, but she had no reasonable explanation why her only instinct, when he kissed her, was to hold on to him. The memory of her hands pinned between her breasts and his bare chest was etched in her mind, the feel of heat and his racing heart under her palms. She stood abruptly, the sensations still so clear to her that she found herself rubbing her hands on the cotton of her T-shirt.

She crossed to the air conditioner and turned it down, then went to the patio doors and opened the closest one. She stepped out onto worn tiles that felt warm under her bare feet, and for a long moment she just stood there. She breathed in the freshness of the desert air and felt the heat of the new day already building.

And all the time she stood there, she was totally aware of Jake's room to her left. As she turned to go

back inside, she glanced over the low wall that separated their patios and saw his doors were all open, just
as Emma had said they would be. Some crumpled
blankets had been discarded on the floor just inside
the door and a pillow was partway out onto the patio.
He didn't use the bed. He slept as close to the open
doors as he could.

She heard a sharp knock on the door to her room
and she hurried back inside. She didn't bother with a
robe as she crossed the room and opened the door.
Emma stood there in jeans and a bright pink shirt that
wasn't tucked in. "Sorry to wake you so early, Miss
Tate, but you've got a call. The man said he had to
talk to you. I told him it was early, but he—"

"I didn't hear the phone."

"I forgot to hook it up in here. Just plug it in the
jack and pick up. I'll put the call through."

"Thanks," Whitney said and closed the door. She
crossed to the bed, found the connection end of the
phone cord, pushed it into the wall jack and a red light
began to flash at the base of the phone. Then she sank
down on the bed, picked up the receiver and pressed
the button. "Hello?"

There was silence, then a click. "Hello?" she said
again.

"Whitney, who in the hell was that woman?" Cutter demanded.

"The manager," she said. "Why?"

"I thought she was going to hang up on me. Actually, I didn't expect to get her. I thought since it was
early there, you'd still be in your room."

"I am. The phone just wasn't hooked up."

"Where's Hill?"

"I don't know exactly. Why?"

"Just find out where he is as soon as you can."

"What's going on?"

"I just contacted Brock Taylor, the head of the company Hill worked for in L.A., and he told me he'd just hung up from talking to Hill."

Whitney glanced at the alarm clock by the phone. Six-fifteen. "Jake called him this morning?"

"Yes. Taylor said it's the first time he's done that. He'd written a few postcards before, but that was it."

"Why did he call?"

"Apparently Taylor said he thanked him for everything he'd done for him, but he was calling to say goodbye, that Taylor wouldn't be hearing from him again."

"I'll say goodbye, Miss Tate," Bob Fillerman had said as he headed for the door of the office by Cutter's. "You won't hear from me again."

As words echoed in her mind, Whitney held the receiver so tightly she felt as if she could snap the plastic. "Did he say why?"

"No. Hill told Taylor not to try and find him. He wouldn't be able to."

She couldn't block Jake's words from last night. *"Life isn't worth the effort."* Whitney felt as if she'd come full circle, and she was watching someone else walk away and never come back. "I'll call you back as soon as I know what's going on." Quickly she hung up and reached for her robe.

She rushed out into the hall and went down to the lobby, but Emma wasn't anywhere in sight. Without stopping, Whitney crossed to the desk, went behind it and stepped through the swinging doors. She found herself in an empty kitchen with a cold black-and-white ceramic tile floor. "Emma!" she called out.

A moment later the woman rushed out of a side door across the room, obviously shocked to see Whitney, but she didn't question her being there. "I knew something was wrong when that man called so early," she said, crossing the floor. "Just tell me what you need me to do."

"I—I..." She stopped, willing herself to sound rational. "I was just looking for Jake."

She frowned. "I suppose he's at the station. I don't know. Why?"

"Did you see him leave this morning?"

"I haven't seen him since yesterday when he brought you here. What's going on?"

She tried to think of a reason for her questions. "I wanted to get to the garage, and I thought he might take me. I guess I could get a taxi."

"There's no taxi in Bliss. We don't even have our own police force. Tell you what, why don't you get dressed. I'll get your breakfast for you, then I can run you to the garage."

"I'm not hungry," Whitney said. "Could you take me now?"

"Well, I suppose so, if you like?"

"I'll be right back." Whitney hurried back to her room. Five minutes later she was in the lobby, wearing white shorts, a blue tank top, sandals and her sunglasses. Gripping her wallet, she was just about ready to call for Emma when the woman came in the front door.

"Ready?" Emma asked.

"Yes, I am."

"Let's go."

Whitney followed Emma outside to an old window van with oxidized green paint and Bliss Hotel Courtesy Van painted on its side, parked at the bottom of the porch steps. Emma got in behind the wheel, while Whitney climbed in on the passenger side. The van started right up. "It doesn't look too good, but it gets me where I have to go," Emma said as she put the van in gear and started down the driveway. "The only thing wrong with it is the air conditioner. Wally hasn't had time to fix it, so we keep the windows down."

Whitney wasn't aware of the growing heat in the air drifting into the van. All she could think of was Jake, finding him, making sure everything was all right. She held tightly to her wallet as she stared ahead.

"Are you sure everything's okay, honey?" Emma asked.

"Yes," she lied, wishing the van would go faster.

"That man on the phone, he acted as if the world was ending. You'd think he owned the world, actually."

"He's like that," Whitney said distractedly as she caught sight of the garage.

Emma turned onto the gravel and headed toward the gas pumps. Whitney got out as soon as the van stopped and hurried across the graveled area to the garage. She stopped when Wally stepped out of the open doors.

"Hello there, little lady. Come to see your car?"

"I—I was looking for..." Her voice trailed off when she saw Jake come out of the dimness behind Wally.

He'd pulled his hair back in a low ponytail. His dark eyes were narrowed, and he was wearing dull gray coveralls smeared with grease and oil. The sight of him standing there made her almost sick with relief and she was thankful for the protection of her sunglasses. She wasn't a good enough actress to cover what she felt right then, what anyone would see in her eyes.

"Jake told you how bad the car was, didn't he, little lady? And you're worried?"

She nodded, unable to think beyond the fact that Jake was here, and he was in one piece. There was no deadly repeat of what had happened with Fillerman.

"Well, don't you worry so," Wally said. "You ought to be able to get your dealer to do the repairs." He motioned behind him to the sports car up on the lift. "No new car should have blown like that, no matter what. My suggestion is to call and—"

"No," she said abruptly, making herself look away from Jake and think rationally. "I...I want you to fix it. If you can, that is."

"But you shouldn't be responsible."

"I'll take it up with my dealer when I get back. For now, I want you to fix it, please."

"All right. We'll do our best, but it's going to be really expensive."

"I don't care."

"It's going to take a while, probably a week at least. I've got to bring in parts for it."

"That will be fine."

Emma came up from behind her. "I filled the van, Wally," she said, then spoke to Whitney. "Do you want me to take you back with me, Miss Tate?"

She shook her head. "No. Thanks." She saw that a restaurant joined to the garage by a breezeway. "I think I'll get some breakfast while I'm here," she said, even though her stomach was still in knots.

"They got good food. Wally's sister runs it."

"Another relative? Is Bliss populated by your relatives?"

Wally shrugged. "Just about. I figure you and Jake are the only two that aren't connected to me and Emma someway."

She glanced back at Jake, but he'd gone back to working on her car. And Cutter was waiting for her to tell him what was going on. "Is there a pay phone close by?"

"If you got to make a call, you can use the phone in there." Wally motioned to the office to the left of the garage. "Just go on in and help yourself."

"Thanks," she murmured and crossed to the office.

In the air-conditioned coolness of the cluttered space, she sat behind the desk, put in a collect call to Cutter and let him know what was going on. As she hung up, she heard a clatter to her left and saw a window right by a door that went out into the garage. Jake was straightening with a heavy wrench in his hand, then he went under the car, looking up as he started to work again.

As Whitney watched him, she finally felt her heart slow to a normal rate and the knots in her middle ease. Jake was here, working on her car. She hated the way she'd reacted to the idea that something could have happened to him. Cutter had told her she wasn't good at this job because she tended to get emotionally involved, yet he'd sent her here.

As Jake backed up and turned to pick up another wrench, Whitney realized that if she wasn't careful she could be more involved with Jake Hill than she had any right to even think about. And that disturbed her a lot.

"Did you get your call made?"

She turned at the sound of Wally speaking and saw him coming in the front door.

"Yes, thanks." She looked back out to the garage. "Is Jake a good mechanic?"

"I think he's pretty damned good."

"Did he have good references?"

She looked back at Wally as he shrugged. "I could tell you he had great references, but I won't." He sat on the corner of the desk and looked out the window into the garage. "Jake showed up here out of no-where four days ago. It was sundown, and he rode in on that bike of his, all chrome and black lacquer, dusty from the desert. He asked for a job, and when I asked for references he said he didn't have any."

She followed his gaze to Jake, who was pulling something off the car. "Why did you hire him?"

"He made me a deal."

"What kind of deal, Wally?"

"He said he'd work for a week for free. If I liked what he did, he wanted the job. If I didn't, he'd leave and I'd get the week for free."

It was Jake's pattern. In the files Cutter had given her, she'd found a part about how he first hired on with Brock Taylor, the head of Waverly International. He told him he'd work for free. When Taylor thought he was worth a salary, he'd take it, or he could show him the door. Taylor had taken the challenge, and so had Wally. "And you're a betting man?" she asked as she looked back at Wally.

His hazel eyes narrowed on her. "That's just what he asked me."

"What did you tell him?"

"That I've been known to cross the state line and head for Vegas from time to time."

"So you took his deal?"

"Yep. He knows cars inside and out."

"You're going to keep him here when the week's over?"

"Now that's the thing. I'd keep him on for a good long time, if I had my way."

"But?"

He shrugged. "There's an old Indian saying around here that a damaged spirit never stops too long in any space. Sad to say, but that man's got a damaged spirit."

Whitney was shocked at Wally's insight. "Why do you say that?"

"I knew it when I first saw him. My father had the same gift, and his father before him. The old one could tell a person's spirit just by looking in their eyes."

She rubbed her arms with the flats of her hands, the room suddenly cool enough to raise gooseflesh on her arms. "A psychic thing?"

He laughed at that. "No, a sort of birthright. It goes through families. Emma says that just because I've got Indian blood, I make too much out of it. But I know what I know." He sobered. "I knew when I let Jake stay that I'd either lose big or win big. I'm edging toward the win myself, but I know that one day I'll look up and he'll be gone."

"He told you that?"

"No, but I've seen men like him before. He's running. Said it's not from the cops, and I believe him. But he's running from something." He cocked his head to one side. "Just why are you so interested in the man?"

She wished she could lie and lie easily. But something about the man made lying seem foolish. "I was just curious," she said, hedging with a partial truth.

"I think while you're here you should take a trip to the burial grounds outside of town. They're set up in the low hills and overlook this whole valley."

"Why should I go there?"

"Because you're a curious girl. It might give you some answers."

"Answers about what?"

"About Jake Hill."

"I said I was curious, that's all."

"Sure. But it's still a good idea to take a run out there, just for curiosity's sake."

A strange uneasiness was creeping into her, and she felt spooked. Damaged spirits and burial grounds were outside of her comfort zone. "All I'm interested in right now is getting some food. I'm going to try the restaurant."

"Make sure you tell Lillian—"

"Your sister?"

"That's her. Tell her I sent you."

She stood and went around the desk to the door. "I'll do that."

"Whitney?"

She turned as she opened the door. "Yes?"

"You never did tell me why you were driving around the desert in the first place?"

The driving vacation lie sounded too hollow to repeat to this man. "You obviously believe in fate."

"Yes, I do."

"Then I guess it's fate of some kind that brought me here."

He smiled at her. "That's not an answer, but I'll let it go for now. Enjoy your breakfast."

Chapter 4

An hour later, Whitney left the coolness of the restaurant and went outside into heat that had to be close
to one hundred degrees. She hurried across to the garage, where the cooling unit suspended from the metal
trusses overhead was trying to battle the building heat.
But as Whitney stepped inside, she knew that the interior temperature was only a bit cooler than it was
outside.

She saw Jake still working under her car on the lift,
and as she got near him he stopped and turned. His
eyes were unreadable, his expression neutral and the
kiss from the night before might never have been.
Whitney could almost believe she'd dreamed it all if it
wasn't still incredibly vivid in her mind. For a heartbeat, she was sure if she touched her tongue to her lips
she would be able to catch his taste lingering there.

"Wally's in the office," Jake said and turned away from her back to his work.

"I wasn't looking for Wally." She moved closer to the car, making a pretense of being interested in what the undercarriage looked like. "I wonder how I could have done that much damage?"

"You probably hit a rock or something on the road and cracked it out."

"How long have you been a mechanic?" she asked as she studied the filthy black soot that covered a good share of the bottom of the car.

"Why do you want to know?"

She turned and found Jake staring at her intently. The directness of his gaze was unsettling, almost as unsettling as the sharp edge to his tone. "You're working on my car, a very expensive car, I might add, and I would like to be sure you're qualified to do it."

She knew he'd love to tell her to drop dead, but he didn't. He held her gaze with his and, as he spoke, he seemed to be daring her to find fault with his answer. "Wally hired me. He knows what he's doing."

"He thinks you're a terrific mechanic."

"Isn't that good enough for you?"

"I don't know." She shrugged. "He also believes in spirits."

"So he's superstitious."

"Did you know he's part Indian?"

"You're just a wealth of trivial information, aren't you?"

"It helps when you're trying to make small talk with people," she said.

His expression tightened perceptibly, and for the first time his gaze faltered. "I suppose I should explain about—"

"No, don't." She held up one hand, palm out. "I just meant that I'm a talker. I always have been. Sometimes it's good, sometimes it's bad. And sometimes I say things I shouldn't. I didn't mean to infringe on anything." Her words were quick, tumbling one over the next, and she took a deep breath. "I definitely make small talk."

Jake hesitated, then unexpectedly his expression eased and she could have sworn a smile played at the corners of his mouth. For once she'd said the right thing with this man. "And I told you, I'm no good at it."

She felt a bit off balance at the change in him, however slight, but it gave her hope that she might be able to break through his protective shell and do her job. "A man of few words?"

"Exactly."

"Wally's not. He's a storyteller."

"He does talk, that's for sure."

"And he seems to like you. He'll be sorry to see you leave. He said he wishes you'd stay more than a week, but he doesn't think you're going to."

She held her breath as she watched a frown suddenly dominate his face, drawing his eyebrows together and blotting out any hint of a smile. "What?"

Hoping she sounded casual, she forged ahead. "Wally said you might not be staying beyond the week."

She'd hoped she could slide into some comment from him about leaving Bliss, about where he'd be going, but that didn't happen. Jake closed down, literally shutting out any expression in his eyes except for a tinge of irritation. "Wally just spilled his guts to you, didn't he?"

"Was it suppose to be top secret or something?"

He shut her out by grabbing a wrench off a roll-away tool chest to his left, then starting to work on the car again.

"Is it true?" she asked, making herself persist, anything to feel as if she was making contact with him again.

He didn't respond for so long Whitney wondered if he was just going to ignore it completely... and ignore her. But just as the silence between them began to make her nervous, he turned, dropped the wrench on the tool chest with a sharp metal-on-metal sound and asked, "What's it to you if it's true or not?"

Lies were hard for her, so she simply backed down. "I was just making conversation."

"And I need to work, or you're going to be stuck in this town forever." He crossed to the central support post and pressed a yellow switch with his thumb. He stared at the car as it slowly lowered to the cement floor, then he let go of the button and glanced at Whitney. "Just what do you want?"

For him to tell her what he was thinking, what drove him to hide in this hot garage when he used to be liaison for an international company. Why he gave up a six-figure income for something that couldn't pay more than six or seven dollars an hour. And why he could disturb her just by looking at her.

"Nothing," she lied. "I was just making small talk."

He studied her from under lowered lashes, his skin beginning to sheen from the heat, then he picked up another wrench. "I think we've been over this subject more than enough."

She could almost feel Cutter at her back, telling her to push, to dig and get the man to say things that could make the difference between life and death for his assignment. So she asked a question that she knew would either blow her out of the water or give her some answers. "You know that Wally thinks you're on the run, don't you?"

She didn't miss the way he clenched the wrench so tightly that his knuckles went white. "He told me."

"Are you?"

He exhaled harshly. "Dammit, lady, you're out of line. This is way past small talk."

She held up both hands in mock surrender. "Sorry. I'm just trying to be a human being."

"Unlike you, I don't have any ambitions to be a so-called human being," he bit out.

"I didn't know we had that choice."

He stared at her hard for a long moment before he shook his head. "That's where you're wrong. I made the choice."

"Why?"

"Maybe for self-protection," he breathed, his voice so low she almost missed the words.

"Did something happen?"

"None of your business."

"Never mind," she murmured. "I'm not going to hold a gun to your head and make you tell me anything."

Words that were chosen carelessly had their impact on Jake. He literally flinched, then he growled, "Son of a—"

The violent curse was cut short when a loud explosion shattered the hot air and rang off the metal walls of the garage. Whitney jerked to her left and saw an old car on the street with black smoke billowing from its exhaust pipe. A backfire. Relieved, she turned back to Jake.

He stood absolutely still, his face devoid of color, the wrench he'd been holding on the floor at his feet. His arms were stiff at his sides, his hands clenched and his eyes closed tightly. The expression on his face exposed an agony that Whitney knew was a living thing in Jake's soul.

The shot from his tormentor's gun echoed in Jake's ears, then the cold metal of the barrel was pressed to his temple. Acrid smoke filled his nostrils, and he didn't move. He knew if he did, there would just be more pain. "Tomorrow, you die." Whispers in the dark taunted him. "Tomorrow, you die."

A voice, soft and urgent, cut through the horror. "Jake, Jake, what's wrong?" The darkness fled, and Jake opened his eyes. He was in the garage, the odors of oil and gasoline were in the air, not gunpowder.

How could it happen? He wasn't asleep. He wasn't alone. One second he was with a woman who was annoying him with her questions, the next he'd heard the gun go off. But it couldn't be. Not a gun. Not at his head.

"Jake?"

Whitney. She'd been the one to draw him out of the darkness. He looked at her by him, not touching him, but close enough so he could see the concern and pity in her eyes. God, he didn't want to be pitied by her, or by anyone.

He ran a hand roughly over his face and exhaled. Reality was all around. And reality was Whitney standing no more than a foot from him, waiting for some explanation.

How could he explain something he didn't understand himself? There were no words in him to justify what had happened, not any more than there had been last night when he'd kissed her. Explanations were painfully elusive and had been for so long he wondered if he'd ever had any answers for anything in his life.

He felt as if he had been given a reprieve when he heard Wally muttering, "That damned Benson kid and his old junk heap. The thing sounds like a cannon when it goes off."

A backfire. Simple. Sane. Wally stepped in front of him, then stooped to pick up the wrench he knew he'd been holding moments ago. He didn't remember dropping it.

Wally held it up. "This yours?"

Jake nodded, his throat tight and painful. He took the wrench and, without looking at Whitney again, turned away from her to put it on the roll-away. He stared blindly at the other tools, painfully aware of the woman close by, and he wished she'd leave, just disappear the way she had last night in the moonlight.

As if in answer to his need, he heard Whitney say, "I'll get out of here and let you two work on the car."

"How about a lift to the hotel?" Wally asked. "The heat's pretty bad right now."

"Thanks, I'll walk. I'll stay in the shade and look around the town a bit on the way."

"If you're sure?"

"I'm sure," she said softly.

When Jake finally turned, Whitney was gone. But not needing to give her answers didn't stop his own need for them. The vision or the episode or the seizure, whatever the hell it had been, was so fresh in his mind that he could swear he smelled the gunpowder.

"Let's get that engine out," he said to Wally, needing to keep busy with his hands so he didn't have to think.

"She's one pretty woman, don't you think?" Wally asked as he went to the car.

Jake shrugged, the tension in his neck and shoulders making a dull ache in his muscles. If he let himself think about Whitney right now, he'd have to admit that "pretty" was hardly an adequate description. And if he'd never kissed her, he might not have tangled up the memories of her taste with the nightmares.

"I hardly know her," he muttered. "But you've been doing some talking to her, haven't you?"

The older man pushed his hat back with his thumb on the brim and eyed Jake. "We talked some. Why?"

"What about?"

"Mostly about fate and spirits."

Jake grabbed a wrench before going over to the car. "Don't start that supernatural mumbo jumbo again."

"I thought you went up to the site yesterday?"

"I did."

"Didn't you find something on the wind, or feel something was in the shadows and quietness up there?"

The man made him uneasy when he talked like this, and Jake was already on edge enough. "Listen, Wally, I don't think—"

"I was just asking what you found," he said calmly. "That's all."

"A lot of emptiness." As soon as Jake said the words, he knew they were a lie. There had been a certain sense of something more than could be seen up there, but he'd figured it was his own ghosts that he seemed to be pulling around with him no matter where he went.

"I'm telling you, if you sit real still and listen, you can hear the old ones talking."

"Sure, and cows fly," Jake said as he reached for the pulley on the engine lift. "Let's get this engine out before it gets as hot as an oven in here."

Thankfully Wally stopped talking, but it only lasted until the engine was clear of the car and securely on its support by the main workbench. "You've got good hands for this job," Wally said. "I hate to see you walk out on me."

Jake cast Wally a sharp look. "What?"

Wally shrugged. "You aren't going to stay after this week's up, are you?"

How did this man and Whitney know what he'd decided before he'd told anyone but Brock? "I'm not good at staying anywhere for very long anymore."

"Some men just can't let go and settle. But do me a favor?"

"What favor?"

"If you find that you don't need to leave, that whatever's driving you will let you sit still for a while, let me know?"

Whatever's driving him? He shut that down, the images skirting the edges of his thoughts, making his nerves raw. "I'll let you know," he said as he rewound the pulley ropes on the hoist.

"You know you won the bet. You got a job here as long as you want one."

"Thanks for that."

"One other thing?"

Jake looked up at the old man. "What?"

"Will you take another run up to the site before you head off?"

He wasn't keen on going back there again. "Maybe. I don't know if I'll have the time to."

"Make the time, son. You need to."

"You really take that Indian thing seriously, don't you, Wally? Things like damaged spirits?"

The old man shrugged his massive shoulders. "Of course I do."

Jake turned back to his work, his hands busy with taking the engine apart, but his mind kept on its own path. No matter what he did, he couldn't block the memory of the look in Whitney's eyes when he'd come out of the nightmare. Or block the fact that it had come to haunt him in the light.

Whitney walked slowly down the wooden sidewalk, barely glancing at the stores and businesses that she passed. Even in the shade of the overhang, the heat was making her skin sticky with moisture, and

without a trace of a breeze the still air had all the uncomfortable qualities of a furnace.

She pushed her hands in the pockets of her shorts,
their unsteadiness a constant reminder of the emotional roller coaster she'd just experienced. She wasn't
trained for this. She never had been. She'd been hired
to debrief released hostages, not to deal with their pain
and trauma. That was dealt with by professionals—
psychiatrists and psychologists.

She knew how to ask questions, not how to deal
with post-traumatic stress disorder. She didn't know
what to do to reach someone lost in their own darkness. And that's where she knew Jake had been. A
backfire from a car, and he'd tumbled down a black
hole where he was totally isolated. No wonder he tried
to keep moving, probably hoping that memories
couldn't catch up with him if he did. He didn't stay
still for long.

She curled her hands into fists in her pockets and
exhaled, blowing air upward to cool her face and ruf-
fle her hair. She was going to get out of this now. She
couldn't handle it, and she couldn't handle the horrible feeling of helplessness as she'd watched Jake. It
made her heart hurt to think about it. The need to
comfort him had been overwhelming, but she'd forced
herself to just talk and not to touch him.

Then she remembered something from dealing with
Bob Fillerman. Touching scared people with PTSD.
Touching was a form of constraint, a way of impris-
oning them, and they feared it. That fear was almost
as great as the fear of remembering. Remembering
could kill. That's what Fillerman had told her that last
day. Memories killed.

She swallowed hard and walked a bit faster. That's just what Cutter wanted Jake to do—remember.

"Hey, Whitney," someone called out to her.

She stopped and glanced around but didn't see anyone stirring on the heat-baked street.

The voice came again. "In here."

Whitney looked to her right, through the open doors of the general store, and saw Emma at the checkout counter near the entrance. When the woman motioned her to come inside, Whitney hesitated. Being around people right now wasn't what she wanted, but she didn't know how to walk away without being offensive.

She took a breath, then went through the open door into coolness where the fragrance of coffee hung in the air and sawdust was scattered on the wooden floor.

"Thought that was you," Emma said. As Whitney came to the end of the counter where a teenage girl finished ringing up the order, Emma asked, "What are you doing walking in this heat? Wally said he'd bring you back later."

"He offered, but I wanted to walk."

"Well, I won't have it. You look terrible, all pale and hot, and positively ready to drop. I'll drive you back to the hotel with me." She turned to the girl who was putting the groceries in a cardboard box. "Reeba, put that on our account."

"Sure thing," the girl said, then finished packing the groceries.

"Do you need anything while we're here?" Emma asked Whitney.

She almost shook her head but stopped when she saw a magazine rack just inside the door. A news

magazine was at the front of a stack, and the cover
caught her attention. It was filled with a black-and-
white head shot of a narrow-faced man with thinning
hair, an ashen complexion and a stunned expression.
Overlaying the photo was the transparent suggestion
of a red clock showing one minute to twelve. A cap-
tion in a box on the right of the black-bordered cover
read High Noon—Hostage Of Terror. Under it was
Ambassador Nelson Winegard.

As Whitney approached the rack, she could make
out the suggestion of swelling at the man's jawline and
a strangely lopsided look to his face. She knew it was
a photo released by the man's captors touched up to
try to conceal the abuse the man had suffered at their
hands.

When Jake had been kidnapped, there had been no
publicity, no pictures on magazine covers. His company had a no-ransom policy, and basically a no-
publicity policy, too. They did what they could to effect his release privately, then they'd finally called in
the government, stipulating no publicity. By then Jake
had been held over four months. Even his escape two
months later, had been kept out of the papers.

With unsteady hands, she picked up the magazine
and stared at the photo. For a heart-stopping moment, Jake's face was in front of her on the cover, his
eyes devoid of hope and mouth clamped shut. Cutter
was right. They had to do whatever it took to get the
ambassador released. Threats of cutting off his fingers or his ears were actually promises. His execution
was a promise, too, if Cutter's people couldn't locate
him and get him out.

Jake's torture a year and a half ago by the same terrorist who had the ambassador had been so horrible that he still couldn't forget. He'd been lucky to escape, but the group wouldn't be careless a second time.

Emma's voice jarred Whitney. "Honey, you getting something?"

"Yes . . . yes, I am." She turned and crossed to the counter to pay the teenager for the magazine. As she followed Emma outside with the rolled magazine in her hand, she knew she'd already accepted the fact that she couldn't quit, she couldn't walk away. She was in this to the end.

When Emma was settled behind the wheel of the old van, she turned to Whitney. "Any preference for dinner?"

Food was the last thing on her mind. "No, whatever you've got is fine with me."

Emma put the car in gear, backed out and turned onto the street in the direction of the hotel. "Since you're the only one, choose what you want."

Whitney looked away from the magazine on her lap. "Pardon me?"

"You've got your pick. No sense in you wanting something I don't have."

"You said I'm the only one?"

"As of this morning, you're my only guest."

"What about Jake?"

"Wally called me just before I came down here and said that Jake's decided he'll just camp out. He says he's not comfortable in the hotel."

Whitney sank back on the hard seat. That put her almost back to square one. The close proximity with

Jake at the hotel was something she'd counted on. "Where could he camp around here?"

"Honey, there's enough open space for anyone to camp anywhere they want to in the desert." She swung onto the driveway for the hotel and came to a stop by the front steps.

Jake's motorcycle was still parked by the hitching post. "What about his bike?"

"He said he'll come get it later."

As Whitney got out, Emma came around to get the groceries and stopped. "Honey, you don't look so good. Are you sure everything's all right?"

She wasn't sure how right anything was just now. "I think I'll go and lie down for a while. I'm not used to this heat."

"Can I bring you something cool to drink?"

"No, thanks." She turned and went into the hotel. Once she'd closed the door behind her after she went into her room, she crossed to the patio entrance, slid the door back and stepped out.

Looking over the low wall, she could see into Jake's room. The doors were shut, but the drapes were open and she could see the bed was made and not a thing was out of place. It looked as if he had never been there. She looked down at the magazine she was still holding in her hands; the ambassador's eyes were the only visible part of his face. With an involuntary shudder, she went back inside and closed the door.

She wasn't going to give up. If Jake wasn't planning to stay at the hotel any longer, she'd change that. One way or another, she wasn't going to let him go off into the desert alone.

* * *

Jake headed back to the hotel at dusk. He'd kept busy all day, but the happenings of the past twenty-four hours had left him edgy and tense. When he walked up the driveway, he scanned the porch area to make sure no one was on the swing, then he headed for the steps.

Wally was taking off for the rodeo grounds in a while to help a friend of his, who owned the set up, to get things ready for the Fourth of July celebration. But Emma was here, so was Whitney, and Whitney was the last person he wanted to see right now. The floorboards squeaked under his boots as he crossed the porch, then he pulled back the door and went inside.

The lobby was empty. "Emma?" he called, but there was no answer. He went across to the back doors and looked out at the central courtyard. The twinkle lights were on in the old olive tree, but there wasn't anyone outside. "Emma?" he called again as he turned to the empty room.

Nothing moved. No sounds beyond the low hum of the air conditioner could be heard. He glanced at the hallway that led to the guest rooms, uneasy with the idea that Whitney could come out any minute. He walked over to the reception desk, then spotted his bedroll and knapsack on the floor behind the desk. He went around, grabbed them, then turned and left.

Once he'd strapped his things on the back of the motorcycle, he got on and tried to start it. But nothing happened. He frowned, fiddled with the key, hit the kick start again and again. But nothing happened. In the gathering dusk he couldn't see very well, so he flipped the kickstand and coasted backward until the light from the porch shone on the engine.

He set the kickstand again, got off and crouched down to study the engine. It didn't take him a second to see that an ignition part was gone, and it hadn't fallen off by itself. He stood and looked around, but no one was in sight.

"All right," he yelled. "Bring it back. No questions asked, just bring it back."

The chorus of insects in the hot night stilled at the sound of his voice, but no one answered him. Anger burned through him, and he raked his fingers through his hair. "Ten bucks," he called out. Nothing. "Twenty!" Still nothing. "Name your price!"

Chapter 5

When there was no answer at all, Jake muttered, "Screw it," and pushed the bike back to the hitching post. Leaving his bedroll and knapsack tied to it, he headed for the porch to go inside and see if he could catch Wally before he left the garage.

As he reached the door, it swung back and Whitney was there. The lights from the hotel were at her back, setting a halo around her delicate figure. "What's going on out here, an auction?" she asked.

"Someone took a part off my bike."

"I thought I heard you yelling something about money."

"Just trying to get it back any way I could. Damn thieves."

"Do you think this is the start of a crime wave in Bliss?" she asked, looking up at him.

He didn't have to see her face to know she thought this was a joke. "It's not funny."

"Of course it's not," she said, stepping past him and onto the porch. He watched her cross to the railing and rest both hands on it as she looked out into the night. "But is it fatal for your bike?"

He knew it was too late to catch Wally now. "No, it's not fatal, just crippling," he said.

She turned to him, and he could see the smile now in the soft light, a gentle, teasing expression that lifted her full lips. "Then you should be thankful. All you need is a tiny part, and your motorcycle will be just as noisy as ever."

He wasn't going to stay out here with her. All he needed was to leave a message with Emma, then figure out where he was going to stay for the night. "Where's Emma?"

"Out where they're doing that rodeo and carnival," she said. "Probably with Wally."

"Who's watching this place?"

"I am."

"You're kidding? You just walked in off the street a day ago, and she left you in charge?"

"The woman who usually takes over, Maria something or other, wasn't around, and Emma wanted to go there tonight to help her friends. Since I'm the only guest here now, I offered to take care of things until she got back."

He moved to the swing and sat down. Leaning forward, he rested his elbows on his knees and looked at Whitney. "She must trust you."

"I suppose so, but I'm not doing too well."

"Why?"

"The great motorcycle robbery."

"I told you, this isn't funny."

"I know it's not. Wally probably has the part you need, don't you think?"

He shrugged. "Probably."

"Then go back and get it from him."

"He's probably headed out to the rodeo grounds by now."

"Then you'll have it tomorrow. That's not so bad. I don't think this is the start of a crime wave in Bliss. Probably just some kid who thought it would be fun."

She couldn't understand that not having the option of getting on the motorcycle made him feel as if he'd been pushed back into "the hole" and locked in. "If that kid was here now, I'd probably kill him."

She cocked her head to one side. "Are you serious?"

"Absolutely. Does that offend you?"

"Not really." Whitney watched Jake and weighed her words carefully. She'd thought about this encounter all day and knew that she'd probably only have one chance to say what had to be said. "It doesn't offend me, but I think that's a particularly ineffective way of dealing with problems in life."

"Oh? What would you do?" he asked, moving the swing slowly back and forth.

"Wait, get the part from Wally, fix it, then do whatever I wanted to do."

"That's very dispassionate."

"It's hard for me to get passionate about a motorcycle part."

"It all depends on what that motorcycle means to a person."

"What does it mean to you?"

She heard him take in a deep breath, then he said, "It's mine. That's enough of a reason to get angry when someone deliberately damages it."

"But would it be worth going to jail and getting locked up for?"

The swing stilled, and even though the light from inside was at his back, she knew Jake was staring at her. Hard.

She deliberately continued. "But maybe you wouldn't mind that. You'd think it was a trade off. Personally, I can't stand being locked up. That feeling of not being able to get air makes me panic. I guess it's a phobia."

As her words died out, the silence between them stretched until Whitney barely breathed. She bit her lip to keep words from coming that would dilute the effect of the ones just said. Then Jake moved, and she was certain he was leaving, but he didn't. He got up and came to the railing by her, gripping it with both hands as he stared down the driveway.

"Have you ever felt like that?" she asked softly. "Not able to breathe, feeling as if you can't take anything into your lungs?"

"Knowing you could die from it?" His words were so low Whitney had to strain to make them out.

"So you've felt like that?"

He exhaled harshly and cast her a slanting look. "I didn't think anyone else had."

"You might be surprised at the number of people who have," she said, knowing the truth of that statement. "People who can't deal with it. People who try to rationalize it or run from it."

He studied her so intently that she knew her cheeks were flaming. Then he spoke in a low, rough whisper, "Who the hell are you, lady?"

"What do you mean?"

"How could someone like you know anything about all of this?"

"Someone like me? What am I like?"

"Someone with money and education and probably a fairy-tale existence."

"That just goes to show you how wrong you can be. I'm not wealthy, just gainfully employed, more by chance than plan, and I've gone to college. As far as a fairy-tale existence goes, that's a crock."

"No Prince Charming?"

There had been men in her life, but none had stayed long enough for her to even begin to think they might be Prince Charming. "Not even close."

"Then what does gainfully employed mean?"

This wasn't what she had in mind, but kept the conversation going with a basic truth. "I'm a statistician."

He looked genuinely taken back. "A what?"

"I compile statistics and form educated opinions about the probability of certain aspects of human behavior being exhibited under relatively predictable circumstances."

He shook his head. "I've heard double-talk before in my life, and that was pure double-talk. Explain that in plain English."

"I gather data about things that happen when people are around other people." A great euphemism for what happened when one human being was terrorized by other human beings.

"Go on."

"Then I put the data together and come up with probabilities for things to happen in any given situation."

"So you predict the future?"

She smiled at that. "No, certainly not. I just do probabilities. I'll leave the psychic things to Wally."

"He's good at it."

"What are you good at?"

He cast her a slanting glance. "Things."

"What things?" she asked.

"Pumping gas, selling tires, fixing cars."

"What about before you did all that?"

"I did the same things, only in a different order."

"You've never done anything else?"

"I've done everything," he said, turning back to the night. "At least once. I could fill your data banks."

"If I had a data bank that covered people who had parts stolen off their motorcycles and how they reacted, I could tell you how other people would react under the same circumstances."

"See who would kill the thief, and who would wait patiently for a part?"

"Exactly."

"Where do you think most people would fall?"

"Ninety-nine percent would wait. You'll wait."

"What makes you so sure of what I'd do?"

"You wouldn't kill anyone."

"How do you know that?"

"You haven't killed anyone, have you?"

He was silent for a long moment, then looked back out into the night and said one word. "Yes."

Whitney stared at him, his profile shadowed and elusive to make out. There hadn't been any mention of a killing in Cutter's file on the man. No mention of death. Maybe she hadn't heard right. "What did you say?"

"I told you I've killed someone," he said just above a whisper.

She looked up at him, trying to read the expression on his face, to see if he was teasing, playing some sort of strange game. But his eyes were shadowed, and his jaw set. "How . . . I mean, what happened?"

"It happened." He turned to her and the light touched his features—the narrowed eyes and clenched jaw. "Leave it at that."

Convincing Emma to go and leave her here hadn't been that easy, but it had been important to be alone when Jake came for his things. Now she wasn't so sure this isolation was a good thing. "Just like that?"

"Just like that."

He moved past her and went down the steps. As she watched, he went across to his bike and took his things off the back. For a moment she was certain he would turn and head down the driveway on foot, but instead he came back. He took the steps in one stride and, standing with his belongings in his hand, he looked down at her. "I guess you're the one I have to see about getting my old room back."

"Sure, I guess so." She ducked her head and went past him into the hotel, aware of him coming behind her. She stopped at the desk to get the key, then led the way down the hallway. After she unlocked the door to his room and pushed it back, she reached in and flipped on the overhead light. Turning, she saw Jake right behind her. "Do you want something to drink or eat? Emma left sandwiches and fruit and some cold drinks."

"Nothing." He went past her into the room, his bedroll bumping her arm.

"Is there anything else you'll need?" she asked from the doorway.

He turned as he dropped his things at his feet, and the artificial light in the room wasn't kind. It cut harsh lines at his mouth and sharp shadows at his cheeks and jaw. "Nothing," he said again.

"Are you sure?"

"I said I'm fine."

She was shaken by a very real need she experienced to do something to ease the tension in his expression. "Maybe some extra towels?"

Abruptly he crossed to her and reached out. For one crazy moment she thought he was going to push her out of the room. But he didn't. He took the key she'd forgotten about, then he gripped the side of the open door, his arm close enough to her shoulder to radiate heat against her skin. "I don't want anything. Your job is over."

She wished it really was over, but it wasn't. And after reading the full story on the ambassador, she knew she couldn't just let Jake push her out the door. She'd been close to something on the porch, so close. Then he'd drawn back. But maybe she could get there again. "Are you sure?"

"Absolutely."

"What about your motorcycle?"

"What about it?"

"What if whoever took that part comes back? Don't you want to hide it or park it someplace safe in case they steal the whole bike next time?"

"I've got the key. If they want to cart if off in a truck, more power to them. I'll get another one. Any more questions?"

His dark eyes were unblinking, and their intensity was disturbing. The next moment she heard herself asking a question she'd thought about for what seemed forever but never intended uttering to him. "Why did you kiss me last night?"

As soon as the words were there, she knew he'd push her out the door and slam it, or he'd tell her to drop dead. And she braced herself.

Jake stared at Whitney. The question stunned him, and worse yet, what answer could he give her? What answer would make sense? As the overhead light exposed the elegant sweep of her throat and the delicate hollow at the base he searched for words. When her tongue darted out to touch her softly parted lips, the answer came from nowhere.

He'd convinced himself he'd kissed her because of a slip in his sanity, because of a painful weakness that the nightmare had exposed, or to simply silence her words that seemed to beat on him. But the real answer was simple. He'd kissed her because he'd wanted to. He'd wanted to touch her and taste her, and, in some way he didn't understand, he wanted to be connected to her. And the idea of a connection with anyone was an unsettling thing.

He let go of the door and turned away from her, crossing the room to the patio doors. One by one he opened them, then took a deep breath of the warm night air. He stood with his back to Whitney, but he could sense her behind him, watching, waiting. "I wanted to stop you from talking." But as his words died out, the lie hung starkly in the silence.

"You what?" she asked.

He stared down at the worn tile floor under his boots. "You heard me."

"You kissed me to make me be quiet?"

He closed his eyes for a moment, then shrugged. "I didn't say it made sense."

She didn't speak for what seemed forever, and Jake finally turned, hoping she'd made it easy on him and disappeared. But she hadn't. She was by the door, just staring at him, then her lashes swept low to veil her eyes and she turned away from him.

Nothing made sense, nothing. And when she closed the door behind her as she left, it didn't make sense that he had a momentary idea of going after her to tell her the truth.

He stared at the wooden barrier, then crossed and turned off the overhead light. In the soft shadows, he caught the scent that seemed to cling to her, the freshness of delicate flowers. "Stupid," he muttered and leaned back against the door. "Damn stupid." And not just for kissing her last night, or the fact that he could still want to tonight if he let himself.

He'd been stupid to tell her about the killing.

The killing. God, he'd put that so far out of his thoughts that he could almost believe it had happened in another life ... in someone else's life.

He tossed the room key on the nightstand, then grabbed his bedroll, undid it and spread it out on the tiles just inside the patio doors. When he sank down on the thick flannel, he tugged off his boots and tossed them to one side. Then he stripped off his shirt, threw it near his boots and took the tie out of his hair to free it around his shoulders.

As he stretched out on the flannel, he stared into the shadows of the ceiling above him and fought the memories that his talk with Whitney had stirred up. But no amount of energy stopped them.

He balled his hand into a fist and hit the floor as hard as he could, but even self-inflicted pain couldn't stop the images that kept growing and solidifying. Nothing could stop them from exploding out of the dark place where he'd hidden them.

The thought of leaving and trying to find some liquor was appealing, but in the next second repulsive. He didn't need blackouts again, or drunkenness where he might dredge up even more ghosts. He rolled on his side toward the open doors and stared at the sky awash with stars. Focusing on a particularly distant one, he breathed deeply and gradually felt his muscles relaxing.

When he felt sleep coming, he almost sat up and tried to shake it off. But it was so inviting, and so needed. Cautiously he let himself go and his last thought was about Whitney by him on the porch, her scent in the air, her body close to his. Then blackness was all around.

Whitney went right past her room and into the lobby. She crossed to the phone on the desk, dialed Cutter's number, then turned so she could keep an eye on the hallway. She didn't want anyone coming up behind her while she talked. After six rings, Cutter answered.

"Yes?"

"It's me."

"How did it go?"

"He's still here."

"The motorcycle—"

"The part you told me to take off put the bike out of commission, but I don't know how long it's going to stay that way."

"Four days."

"If Wally has another part, he'll be gone tomorrow."

"You've got four days. Trust me. The part he needs won't be available *anywhere* until after the Fourth of July holiday. I'll make sure so forget about that. Concentrate all your attention on Hill."

She couldn't remember when she'd thought about anything else but Jake. One way or another. "Do you remember hearing anything about him killing someone?"

"There's no record of it. Why?"

She turned and looked around the deserted lobby. "He said he did."

"Who? When?"

"I don't know. I thought it might have been when he was in the service or at one of his jobs before he met Brock Taylor."

"I'll find out for you. Meanwhile, keep at it. It sounds as if you're getting close to him."

She shut her eyes tightly, the thought of being any closer to Jake, disturbing. "He'll talk to me, if I keep at it."

"Good. I'll be in touch," he said and hung up.

Whitney put the receiver back on its cradle, then crossed the lobby to the back doors. Stepping out into the night, she headed for the benches near the olive trees where she could keep an eye on the entrance. As she sank down on the warm wood, she realized she had an unobstructed view of Jake's room, too.

The lights were out, the doors all open and nothing stirred. She almost crossed to make sure he was still there but stopped herself. There was nothing she could do to keep him from walking off into the desert if he chose to. Curling up in the corner of the bench, she hugged her leg to her breasts and rested her chin on her knees.

He was in "the hole," the stench of sewers and filth mingling horribly in the fetid air of the tiny space. He was naked on the dirt. The door lock jiggled, and the rusted hinges groaned. Then a brilliant light flooded in. He staggered to his feet, blinded by the glare. Someone was there, wrapping a smelly rag around his eyes. He was shoved backward against the rough wood of the walls and splinters cut into his bruised back.

The voice, the only one he'd heard in six months, was a hot whisper in his right ear. "American pig, you die." The cold barrel of a gun pressed at his temple. "Die!" Click. The man laughed, a crazy, high-pitched sound, then the gun was at his chest, cutting into the skin over his heart.

Another click reverberated. Another reprieve. More laughter as the gun jabbed at his head again. Suddenly it happened again, him knowing that the third time the chamber would be full. He would die. But he

*wouldn't die without fighting and taking someone
with him.*

*His scream cut through the darkness, torn from his
soul. He scrambled forward, then twisted and swung
violently to his right where he thought the man with
the gun stood. He felt his hand strike flesh. He twisted
again, flailing with his hands until he had his tormentor by his arms and the two of them fell backward onto the floor.*

*With weight over him, he wanted to kill, to throttle
the life out of the man before his own life was stopped.
The killing. His hands were at the man's throat, and
he knew death would come. Then he would run and
keep running until he was in air that could be
breathed.*

"No, please," someone gasped. "Jake, please, stop.
Please."

He froze. It was wrong. The dream was gone. The
voice was different. "The hole" was gone, and its rank
odors were replaced by the sweetness of the desert
night and an achingly delicate scent of warmth and
flowers.

In one heartbeat he knew where he was, on his back
on the floor in his room. Above him, in the soft light
from the night outside, he saw Whitney, both of her
hands grasping at his, fighting to free herself from his
stranglehold at her throat.

Her eyes were wide with fear, a fear of him, and he
could feel her pulse beating frantically under his
hands. He jerked back, letting her go, and she half fell
to his left and away from him. He pushed back,
scrambling until he was sitting, pressed back against

the doorjamb. Whitney was on her knees, her hands braced on the floor, her head down, gasping for air.

His heart hammered against his ribs, and the knowledge he could have killed her made him physically sick. "Oh, God," he whispered hoarsely, swallowing sickness that rose in his throat. "Are...are you all right?"

She sank back on her heels, one hand still at her throat, and her eyes met his. "I..." She swallowed, then managed in a raspy voice, "It's all right."

But it wasn't. He could have killed her. His life, which had been something to endure, suddenly became something terrifying. He could have damaged the only thing of beauty he'd experienced in what seemed an eternity.

He moved forward, inches from her, and impulsively he reached out, needing to let her know his touch didn't mean pain. Sickness rose again when he saw her flinch at the contact, but he didn't draw back. With unsteady fingers, he touched her hand at her throat, the silky skin so vital that it took his breath away.

She never took her eyes off him, her gaze shadowed by incredible lashes. "I'm so sorry," he breathed.

He drew back and stood, but his legs were unsteady and he reached for the door frame for support. He looked out at the courtyard, the twinkle lights a silent mockery after what had almost happened.

"Why are you in here?" he asked.

"I was in the courtyard and I...I heard a scream," she said in a low, hoarse voice out of the shadows behind him. "What happened?"

"A dream."

"What was it about?"

"Things," he said, and heard her move. Suddenly she was right behind him, her scent in the air all around him.

"What things?" she breathed.

He closed his eyes. "Ugly things." He turned, knowing she was close, but not prepared for the impact the sight of her in the soft shadows of night in his room would have on him. Or for the way his heart ached when he saw her hand move from her throat to her shoulder.

He'd hit her. He remembered the blow, and it had been her. And he could still feel her throat in his hands, the way her pulse beat frantically from fear.

"If I was you, lady, I'd get the hell out of here and keep going."

She didn't move. "Tell me what happened," she said softly.

"Didn't you hear me?" he rasped. "For God's sake, I could have killed you."

"You didn't. But you owe me an explanation."

He turned away from her, raking both hands through his hair, then he clasped his fingers behind his neck. "I was dreaming. I thought...I got mixed up and thought you were someone else, someone out of the dream."

"Who did you think I was?"

He dropped his hands and exhaled harshly. "Don't you ever give up?"

The heat of her breath brushed his bare skin, and his whole body began to respond involuntarily to her closeness and the needs that were growing more and more defined with each passing second. "You can say I'm persistent, stubborn if you want."

He literally held his breath, waiting, afraid to move in case he turned and reached out for her.

"Did it have anything to do with the killing?" she asked softly.

Chapter 6

Jake flinched internally at her choice of words, "the killing."

"I had a nightmare about...that time. And I couldn't stop it."

"Who did you kill?"

If only Whitney would stop and go away, then he could leave and keep walking until the ugliness would slip back into some dark crevice of forgetfulness. But she didn't leave. So he made himself move away from her. He went forward, out the doors and onto the small patio.

Night insects were raucous on the warm air, and even though Jake was outside, he could feel that suffocating sensation in his chest when he couldn't breathe right. He never talked about this, never. He thought he'd forgotten, until the words came out on the porch earlier. Now it was all there, every destructive detail.

"I don't know what his name was," he admitted in a low voice. "I actually only saw him once, but I'll never forget him." The image of the man laying dead at his feet at the door of "the hole" was burned into his mind. Eyes wide with surprise, the swarthy face twisted in death. Not a monster, as he'd thought during those six months, just a man who had passionately believed in the expendability of another man's life for the sake of the cause.

"He had this laugh, high and strange." Jake was braced for the words to bring the horror, for the images to take over, but they didn't. He moved to the low wall and pushed his hands deep into the pockets of his jeans. "I hated that laugh."

Whitney stayed at the door, watching Jake, never taking her eyes off him. A trick of the night shadows made crisscross blurs on his bare back, and his shoulders were hunched forward. Slowly he rocked back and forth on the balls of his feet, moving, always moving, as if he believed that to stop would to be lost in the horrors again.

Horror. Her throat ached and burned, and her heart was still beating faster than normal. She'd tried to help him, to make him wake from the nightmare, then he'd struck out, hitting her in her shoulder. When she'd tried to grab him, he'd seized her by the throat and fear had been her all-consuming emotion.

She'd begged him to stop even as her air was being cut off, and suddenly he'd been there, in the room and out of the horrors that had gripped him. His eyes had shown such a misery that everything had changed.

Any fear of him had gone, replaced by a need to comfort him that was overwhelming. Without touching him, she had to be there. She wasn't about to leave him alone with his monsters. So she kept talking, prodding into his darkness with her questions. "And you killed him?"

"I beat him, then I strangled him," he admitted in an oddly flat voice.

She stopped herself from touching her throat, and she pushed back the memory of that moment. "Why did you do it?"

"He was going to kill me. I had to beat him to it."

She knew then how Jake had escaped. In Cutter's papers there was no mention of his method of getting free, just the fact that he'd shown up at the American embassy in Ankara, Turkey. He killed one of the terrorists who had guarded him, and no doubt tortured him. And as surely as she was with him now, she knew that Jake hadn't told anyone about it before.

"So you *did* beat him to it?"

"Barely." She could see him take a deep breath. "He's dead. I'm alive. That's the bottom line."

She stepped out of the room onto the warm tiles of the patio to go closer to Jake. He was alive, but that life was filled with pain and uncertainty. "You were protecting yourself, and it's over. It's in the past."

"Sure it is," he muttered.

"It is." She went closer to him, but stopped when she could see his back more clearly. What she'd thought were tricks of shadows before were scars that marred his back in a haphazard pattern. An ache in her middle seemed to spread through her body, and her hand raised of its own volition. Unsteady fingers touched a scar that echoed the line of his shoulder blade.

Jake jumped at the contact, turning sharply. "Don't!" he gasped.

She drew her hand back. "Did he do that to you?"

He was very still. "Get the hell out of here."

She held her ground. "I told you—"

Her words were cut off when he reached out and grabbed her by her shoulders. His fingers dug into her flesh, and she could feel him trembling. "I'm warning you to leave now. I'm not fit for you to be around."

"Don't say that, you—"

He shook her once. "What's wrong with you? Don't you get it? I had my hands around your throat. I was going to kill you. Dreams, nightmares, visions or demons. I don't know. But I was going to kill you!"

"But you *didn't*."

His face twisted with an agony that broke her heart, and she reached out, touching his chest with her hands. The beating of his heart was under her palms, and all she wanted to do was take away the pain.

"For God's sake, lady, run," he whispered. "Now."

"No." The single word stood between them, then she felt his hold on her ease.

His hands shifted, touching her neck, but this time there was no threat in them. His fingers trembled on her skin, and he whispered, "You're so delicate. So vulnerable. I never wanted to hurt you. I never . . ."

She touched her finger to his lips. "I know. I understand."

His lids lowered, his gaze shadowy, but the edge of pain was there. "No, you don't," he breathed hoarsely. "I don't even understand it."

His hands shifted, and as he uttered a low groan that sounded almost desperate, he pulled her to him. His arms surrounded her, holding so tightly that he trembled as he pressed his face against her hair.

She knew he needed someone, anyone, to hold on to, and she was here. With her cheek against his heart, its wild beating in her ear, she waited. His essence surrounded her, a maleness mingled with heat and fresh air, and she let herself go. She got lost in sensations, with no idea how long they stood like that before he slowly eased back.

His arms were still around her, and as she opened her eyes, she tipped her face to look up at him. In a single heartbeat, all of her selfless motives were blown away. Every atom of her being responded to the man whose body was pressed to hers. Her breasts barely touched his bare chest, but she could feel them swelling through the cotton of her top.

She saw a pulse beating rapidly in the hollow of his throat, and her mouth went dry. Something she realized she'd felt from the first moment he rode up to rescue her on his motorcycle hit her full force. With his body against hers, Jake stirred her on such a basic level that she had trouble assimilating it.

She knew she probably should have done what he'd told her to do. She should run and keep running, but not because of any physical threat he posed to her. Because she could want so much more than to just be here for him, to let him lean on her and hold on to her.

Heat suffused her body, and an ache knotted in her middle. She had to leave, she knew that, but before she could make herself move, Jake leaned toward her and his mouth found hers. The first kiss was nothing compared to this contact. Heat and need exploded in her, a white-hot searing of her soul, and she clung to Jake. Need and passion intermingled, creating something that she couldn't even name. Something she had never experienced before.

She willingly parted her lips, inviting his invasion, and his taste seemed to be everywhere. Reality had no place in the desert night. No man had ever touched her this way, bringing a passion to her that literally took her breath away. There was no Cutter, no lies, just a searing need for a man she barely knew. Yet a man she could love as surely as she knew she could breathe.

Jake ravished her, her ache growing into an agony that was as exquisite as it was disturbing. When his lips left her mouth to burn a path along her jaw to her throat, the moan that echoed in her ears was her own. She arched her back, pressing her hips against his, feeling the hardness of his own wanting against her.

His hands framed her face as his mouth met hers again, and she stood very still, letting the feelings wash over her. She'd never thought that time could stand still, but right then she would have wished it could forever. She wanted that moment to be sealed in time, to be relived over and over and over again.

His hands swept down her throat, skimming over her skin, sending flares of ecstasy through her. Then he touched her shoulders and a sudden pain in her right shoulder made her gasp.

Jake moved back when Whitney gasped, and in the low light he saw the darkening of a bruise at the crown of her shoulder. A grim imperfection on her silky skin, and he'd done it when he'd hit her during the nightmare. He'd held her, selfishly taking what she offered to anchor him and hold back the nightmares. He'd let himself think he could touch her and kiss her, but what he knew he could do was hurt her. And that scared him more than anything had before.

He drew back, breaking all contact with her, aching for the feel of her under his hands, yet remembering the feeling of the impact when he'd struck out. "Get away from me," he rasped. "For God's sake, get out and stay away."

She stared up at him, her lips parted, her eyes wide. He wanted fear back in her eyes, not this softness. "Jake, we can talk," she said, reaching out for him with her hand.

He jerked away before he could feel her touch on him again. "Talking won't do any good. Do you think I can control my demons? Do you think I can will them up, then banish them with a word? I can't!"

He was yelling, his voice echoing all around him, yet she stood in front of him, unmoved, watching. And he was sure she was waiting for him to stop before she started her rationalizing again. "I had my hands around your neck," he rasped.

"It wasn't me you wanted to strangle."

He shook his head, his eyes burning painfully, and he made himself stare at her shoulder. "Whoever it was, I hurt you. And I will again." The stark statement hit him in the gut, and he knew he was the one who had to get out of here. He had to breathe and not inhale her fragrance. He had to move and not be terrified of touching her.

He went past her into his room, being careful not to come close to her. Quickly he pushed his feet into his boots, then grabbed his T-shirt and went back to the patio. Whitney hadn't moved. He stepped past her, without looking at her, and started for the low wall.

"Jake, where are you—"

"I'm out of here."

"But your motorcycle—"

"I'll walk," he muttered, his back to her. There was no way he could look at her.

"You don't have to go," she said. "I'll leave you alone."

The word "alone" cut through him. Alone. Absolutely and totally alone.

"Jake," she said from behind him, the hope that she'd really leave crushed at the sound of her voice. "I just wanted to say that if you need help—"

He turned on her, the cotton of the T-shirt crushing in his hands. "Dammit, I don't want help! I just need . . ."

His voice lost its power as moonlight bathed her face, shadowing her eyes, but not hiding the pity directed at him. "What *do* you need?" she asked in a whisper.

He'd never needed anything or anyone in his life, and suddenly he knew if he let himself relax, if he let down his guard, he could want her with an intensity that would rob him of all reason. And he knew that was totally impossible. "I need to know you're out of here and safe."

"I'm going, but I'll be here if you want... anything," she said softly.

His eyes burned. His throat ached and he did the most unselfish thing he could ever remember doing in his life. He turned away from her and said a lie of monumental proportions. "I don't need anything from you."

He closed his eyes and waited, expecting her to come back with a rejoinder challenging his statement. Then he heard the door to his bedroom open and close. He didn't have to turn to know Whitney was gone. The emptiness behind him caused a chill that no amount of desert heat could dispel.

Whitney felt as if she'd been blindsided. Her legs were weak and her hands trembled as she walked down the hallway to the lobby. If she'd been shaken by the incident with Jake at the garage, she'd been devastated by what had just happened in his room.

She tried to sort out her feelings, but nothing settled into rational slots. Nothing. Her roller coaster of emotions had gone from concern, to fear, to compassion, to need, to passion, to wanting desperately to help. And she couldn't deal with any of them.

In the lobby, she sank down in one of the chairs near the adobe fireplace and pulled her knees up to her chest. Wrapping her arms tightly around her legs, she rested her forehead on her knees and tried to breathe evenly.

She knew pretty much what Jake had gone through in captivity. She'd listened to enough debriefings of hostages to not be shocked by what their captors had done to them. But none of it had touched Whitney the way Jake had. The pain in his expression, the scars on his back, his fear of being with anyone.

Her offer of help had sounded so mundane when she'd said it, but she knew she'd do anything to help him. She knew Cutter didn't have any qualms about calling in markers. Surely someone with expertise in helping PTSD victims owed him something, someone who wouldn't get so emotionally involved with the man, who could think past wanting to hold on to him and comfort him. Someone whose presence wasn't based on lies.

This had all started out as one big lie. Lies had been the foundation of her being in Bliss, and lies had been the reason she'd been here when Jake had the flashbacks. She swallowed, the tightness lingering in her throat. It wasn't Jake's fault, none of it was.

She hadn't realized anyone else was in the lobby until someone startled her by touching her shoulder. She jumped and looked up, incredibly relieved to see Emma standing over her and not Jake.

Emma looked hot and tired, with dirt smearing her face, staining her hands and soiling her jeans and loose top. "Honey, you could have gone to bed. I should have told you to just lock the front door and listen for the bell."

"I wasn't sleepy," Whitney said, sinking back into the chair.

"Well, I'm ready to sleep. I'm getting a bit old for all that tent-raising stuff. I sure wouldn't do it for anyone but Les and Grace."

"They're your friends?"

"Yes. They own that show—lock, stock and barrel, as the saying goes. But it's a day-to-day business.

Sometimes they do real good, and sometimes they're short, like they are now. By the end of the summer, they'll be set for a while.''

"Are they from around here?"

"Born and raised, just like me and Wally. We all went to high school together. Years and years and years ago." She barely covered a yawn. "Which reminds me of my age. I'm beat."

Whitney stood, thankful that her legs felt more steady than they had been moments ago. "I'm tired, too." She wondered if she'd be able to sleep without her own nightmares tonight. "I think I'll go to bed."

"Thanks again for watching things while I was gone. I hated to put that on you, but Maria was off at her sister's place. She'll be here tomorrow."

Whitney brushed at her hair, smoothing it back from her face. "You're going to be gone tomorrow?"

"I'm going back out to help. They aren't nearly done." She started for the front door and spoke over her shoulder. "It's actually kind of fun, getting involved like that. Besides, it only happens once a year." She locked the door, then crossed to the desk. Hitting a bank of light switches, she turned off all the overhead lights, leaving on two side lamps by the entrance. "I noticed Jake's bike out front. What's going on?"

"Someone stole a part off the motorcycle." Lies just seemed part and parcel of her time here.

Emma shook her head. "Those damned kids. School's out and there's nothing to do until the rodeo starts up."

"Since Wally wasn't here, Jake decided to stay for the night. I gave him his old room. I hope that's all right with you."

"It makes my life simpler. Wally wanted me to find Jake at the station first thing in the morning and ask him to go out to the carnival. Les has got a ride that's not working right, and Wally thought Jake could fix it."

"What about the garage?"

"Wally got the Grover kid to go in and pump gas. They can't do any more on your car until they get the parts, and there's nothing there that's an emergency." She yawned again and shook her head. "I'm off to bed," she said, going behind the desk to the swinging doors. "Thanks again."

"No problem," she said.

After Emma had gone into her private quarters, Whitney turned and went to her room. As she stepped inside and closed the door, she stood in the shadows, listening. But she didn't hear anything over the low hum of the air conditioner. Either Jake was asleep, or he'd taken off into the desert.

She crossed to the bathroom, stripped off her clothes and turned on the shower. Without waiting for the water to heat up, she stepped under the cool spray. Shivering, she let the water cascade over her, then as it warmed, she lifted her face to the stream. It was just too bad that the water couldn't wash away the feel of Jake's hands on her, his lips on hers or the horror of the scars on his back.

Sleep for Whitney that night was little more than scattered naps interspersed with disjointed dreams.

When she finally gave up and sat up in the tangled mess of linen, the clock read 6:18. She'd never been a morning person, yet the past two days she'd been up at dawn. She stretched her arms over her head, easing tension that lingered in her neck and shoulders, then swung her legs over the side of the bed.

Through the closed patio doors, she could see the old olive tree backdropped by a sky awash with the palest of pinks and purples. The leaves ruffled with a morning breeze and Whitney wondered how long it had stood there, unmoving, steadfast, surviving through anything and everything.

It was too bad people weren't like that. Too bad they had their limits. She shivered involuntarily and stood, blocking off the question that followed it. How close was Jake to his limit? She padded barefoot into the bathroom and crossed to the pedestal sink. Gripping both sides of the porcelain with her hands, she looked in the oval mirror.

The bruise at her shoulder seemed paler this morning, a slight discoloration. She prodded it with her fingertips, but the pain wasn't too bad. As she combed her hair back from her face with her fingers, she lifted her chin and exposed her neck. She didn't know what she expected, but the only sign of Jake's hands on her neck were two small bruises by her windpipe and a slight abrasion under her left ear.

She touched the marks with the tip of her finger, then reached for her makeup case. Quickly she dabbed coverup on the marks and blended the liquid, then she got dressed in white shorts and a blue tank top. After she ran a brush quickly through her feathery hair, she went back into the bedroom.

When the phone rang, it startled her. Going to sit on the mussed bed, she reached for the receiver. "Hello?"

Emma's voice over the line. "It's that man again. I told him you're probably asleep, but he insisted, so—"

"It's all right. I was up. I thought you were going to the fairground?"

"I am as soon as Maria gets here. Do you want the call put through?"

"Yes, please."

"All right. Here he is."

The line clicked, beeped twice, then Whitney could tell someone was on the line. "Cutter?"

"Getting past that woman is harder than getting in to see the president," he muttered.

"I'm not the president," she said. "And it's only just after six o'clock here."

"I thought you'd want to know what I found out about Hill."

She closed her eyes. "What did you get?"

"There isn't any record of him being involved in a homicide or even involuntary manslaughter. I've got a feeling he was playing with you, doing mind games."

She wished that was it. "Cutter, he killed his guard, or at least one of the men who held him hostage. He strangled him. He said he had to, that it was just a matter of time before they killed him."

"Damn," Cutter breathed, his annoyance at being out of the loop very obvious. "He never said a thing about it when my people first talked to him, just that he'd made a break for it and got free."

"It wasn't that simple." She lay back on the bed and stared up at the ceiling. "He didn't give me any details, but at least he's talking."

"Is he going to stick around for a while?"

"I don't know. He'll probably be here until the motorcycle's fixed. And I think he has a kind of sense of obligation to Wally, his boss. I think he'll stick out his week before he heads out."

"I'll just block the motorcycle part a bit longer."

"No." She said the word before she thought it out. But she knew she was right. "Don't do that. If he's going to tell me anything, it's going to be in the next day or two." She closed her eyes and rested her forearm over her them. "Any news about the ambassador?"

"No new messages. The terrorist group, The Light of Man, has dropped off the face of the earth, along with the ambassador. But the deadline's still in place."

"I saw the piece in *News Time*. You're being pretty up-front about it."

"No reason to keep the facts quiet."

"There wasn't anything on Jake, was there?"

"Taylor wanted it that way. He'd do anything for the man, but he was worried about what it would do to his company connections over there if it got out."

"I guess profit and loss are the bottom line, even when you're negotiating for a man's life."

"Welcome to reality, Whitney."

She'd found reality last night and it had hit her right between the eyes. "Thanks," she muttered with a tinge of sarcasm. Then she heard a door open and close and she sat up. "I have to go."

She hung up and crossed to the door. Quietly she turned the knob, then eased back the barrier to look outside. All she could see was Jake heading down the hall. She hurried to put her sandals on, grabbed her room key along with some money and sunglasses, then went out into the hall.

It was empty now, but she could hear Emma talking. Pushing the key and money into her pocket, she hurried down the hall and out into the lobby. She stopped just inside the room. Jake was by the desk talking to Emma, and Whitney had a chance to just look at him.

He wore the usual white T-shirt and worn jeans with his cowboy boots, and his hair was caught in a low ponytail. As he slipped his faded baseball cap on, he turned, and for a moment Whitney saw something in his eyes. But before she could begin to define it, he put on his sunglasses.

"Good morning," Emma said with a smile. Then her expression faltered. "What happened to you?"

Whitney didn't understand until she realized the woman was staring at her shoulder. The bruise. She'd forgotten about it, more worried about covering the marks on her throat. "Oh, I . . . I knocked into the door," she said.

Jake spoke abruptly. "I'll wait for you in the van, Emma."

"Sure. I'll be out in a minute." As Jake crossed to the door and disappeared outside, Emma closed the top on a wicker basket sitting on the desk. "Do you need me to get you anything for that bruise?"

"No, it's fine." She crossed to the desk. "Did Maria get here okay?"

"Yes, she just arrived, so Jake and I are getting a late start. What do you have planned for today?"

She knew right then what she was going to do today. "I was thinking, if it's all right with you, I'd just tag along and see if there's anything I can do to help out there."

Emma shook her head. "Honey, that's sweet, but this is your vacation, and it's bad enough your car's all broken down. You don't want to be doing work, too."

"I've never seen how a rodeo and carnival are run. If I won't be in the way, I'd like to go with you."

"Goodness, you wouldn't be in the way at all. But I don't know—"

"Emma, there isn't much to do around here, and I hate television."

"Sure, why not. You're on." She reached for keys on the desk. "If you get bored or it's too hot, someone can run you back here. How's that?"

"That's great."

"Do you need anything before we leave?"

"No, I'm all set."

She picked up the basket and came around the desk. "Maria, we're leaving!" she called out, then headed for the door.

As Whitney followed her out, she slipped on her sunglasses and crossed the porch. Jake was already in the van in the passenger seat, the window down and his arm resting on the metal frame.

Even with his sunglasses in place, she didn't miss his surprise when Emma opened the side door for her to get in. She sat on the bench seat behind the driver, tugged the window open, then sat back. One glance at Jake and she knew if she'd said she was coming inside, he would have backed out. Now he stared out the open window, figuratively turning his back on the occupants of the van.

Emma started the van and headed down the driveway to the street. "Got to tell you two, it's going to be a big help to have extra hands out there." She glanced at Jake. "Sorry about your bike, but I'm sure Wally'll have a part for it. He's got a bit of everything."

"I hope so," Jake said in a low voice without turning, his left hand open, pressed to the denim that encased his thigh.

Whitney stared at his hand, the strong fingers with short, square-tipped nails, and a sprinkling of dark hair on the back. Hands that had turned her blood to fire last night, and hands that had encircled her throat. She turned from the sight to look out the window to her left, and she barely covered an involuntary shudder.

A man she barely knew, a man who had warned her to stay away from him, could make her mouth go dry and her heart hammer in her chest as if she was some teenager in the throes of a crush. The same man had confessed to killing another man.

Chapter 7

Whitney swiped at her face, at moisture beginning to dot her skin. "How far is the fairground?" she asked.

"You could walk it if you had to," Emma said. "It's not more than two miles."

Whitney stared at the desert that stretched far to the west, the clear light of morning cutting sharp contrasts on the buttes off in the distance. "Where are the burial grounds that Wally's been talking about?"

Emma laughed. "He's been filling your head with his stories about that place?"

"He was telling me a bit about it."

"That means he talked your ear off," Emma said as Whitney glanced at the rear-view mirror and met the woman's smiling eyes. "They're the other direction out of town, maybe two miles down the main highway, then five or six miles into the low hills."

"What's it like up there?"

"It's a mesa of sorts, maybe a mile across, with high walls on three sides, and a view of this valley to the west. The actual burial site's on a rise near the middle with some partial markers. Its perimeter is lined by stones, and all that's left of the entrance are two pieces of wood that used to be an arch of some sort. No one goes onto the actual burial area, but you can look around outside the stone ring, and there's what's left of a mining attempt that was stopped when the local tribe got some court order to stop desecrating sacred land.

"There's not much there for tourists, that's for sure. Sand and rocks and coyotes. Wally makes treks there every so often. Soothing his soul, he calls it."

"Have you gone there?" she asked.

"Sure, lots of times. Before you ask, I've never seen a ghost or heard any. It's sort of eerie, actually, but Wally feels it's a spiritual place, that whoever goes there gets what they need." She glanced at Jake. "Jake, you've been there. Did you see any ghosts?"

"None that talked to me," he murmured without looking at her.

"That's what I figured," Emma said, then, "We're here."

Whitney looked ahead to a dusty area off to the right ringed by a scattering of runted trees and defined by temporary chain-link fencing all the way around. The entrance, wire gates on either side of a ticket office in a small trailer that had been painted with an American flag, was spanned by a twenty-foot-high wooden horseshoe painted gold and decorated with a banner—Jessop's Rodeo and Carnival. Down the fence stood a truck trailer with a faded mural of a cattle drive on its side, and on the far end was an old motor home.

As they got closer and Emma pulled into the dirt parking area, Whitney could see half-erected game booths, an old Ferris wheel, bumper cars, some kiddie rides, a fun house made from a trailer with a false front and lots of dust. Beyond the carnival, a pipe-fence rodeo arena was ringed by horse trailers and pickup trucks. Livestock pens, and a large dirt roping area with portable bleachers, were just beyond it.

A dozen or more people were toiling in the heat, erecting a huge red-white-and-blue tent in the middle of the carnival section, and others were on ladders, stringing what looked like lights from booth to booth. As Emma pulled in by the trailer at the fence, Whitney slid the side door back and got out into the blanketing heat. She heard Jake get out, his feet hit the hard ground, and she saw the dust rise around her.

Then Emma came around and spoke to Jake. "Let's find Wally and see what he needs." She glanced at Whitney. "Find some shade, hon, and I'll be back in a minute."

Whitney watched Jake and Emma walk through the front gates, and before they got to the tent Wally came out to meet them. His face was flushed, his shirt already damp and sticking to him, but the black Stetson was firmly in place with a bright red feather in the hatband.

She watched him hug his wife, then with his arm around her, he talked to Jake. After a moment, he let go of Emma, slapped Jake on the shoulder, then pointed to the Ferris wheel before heading for it with Jake.

Whitney looked away and leaned back against the van. Jake had acted as if she didn't exist. He hadn't looked at her after that first time, and didn't acknowledge her when he left with Emma. Not that she was surprised by that, not after what he'd said last night, but she was surprised by the discomfort in her that whatever tenuous connection might have begun to forge in his room had shattered.

"Whitney?"

She looked up as Emma came toward her accompanied by a thin woman with dark, gray-streaked hair caught in two braids and pulled back from a high-cheekboned, tawny-skinned face. The woman wore jeans along with an off-the-shoulder white blouse, and Whitney didn't doubt that the woman had to have some Indian blood.

"Whitney Tate, meet Grace Jessop."

Whitney smiled at the woman. "Hello."

"Emma said you wanted to help."

"Yes, I do."

"Great, we can use extra hands today. But I hope you'll be back tomorrow evening to see this place the way it should be seen."

"I'll make sure she gets here, Grace. It's part of the hotel's hospitality to make sure that both of our guests get to the Fourth of July celebration."

"I'd love to come." Whitney glanced around. "I've never seen anything like this before."

"Then you're not a small-town girl?" Grace asked.

"No, I'm not. Not even close."

"For Les and me, this is like our child." She waved one hand to encompass the whole area. "Right now it doesn't look like much, but when it's all set up, when the sun goes down and the lights come on, it's magical. Especially the big wheel. Red, white and blue, slowly going around and around. It's great. That's why we were so glad that Wally got that young man to help with the motor. It would be a shame if the wheel wasn't working tomorrow night."

"Jake's a wonder with anything mechanical—at least, that's what Wally's told me," Emma said. "And Whitney's willing to do whatever you want done."

"Just tell me what you need," Whitney said.

Grace motioned for the two women to follow her, then started for the gates. "What I need is to get the tent finished. The men are almost done with anchoring it, but we have to help with the panels and the inside."

Whitney went through the entrance, and as she walked with Grace and Emma toward the massive tent she looked off to her right and saw Jake by the Ferris wheel. He was on his haunches with two other men, studying a huge motor by the wheel. The other men were shirtless, but Jake had his T-shirt on, the cotton sticking to his back like a second skin.

She stopped at the entrance to the tent, the flashing memory of the healed scars marring his skin, making her stomach clench. When she turned, she was surprised to find Grace right by her, the other woman staring at Jake, too. "So you feel it, too?"

Emma went off to help a young boy uncoil heavy ropes near a stack of wood, and Whitney looked at Grace. "Feel what?"

"The trouble in that man." She met Whitney's gaze with dark, serious eyes. "Wally was telling me about him, and when I met him I knew Wally was partly right."

"He was right about what?"

"About him running." Her gaze slid past Whitney and she knew Grace was looking at Jake again. "He's running, but not away from something," she said softly. "He's running toward something, looking for something." She looked back at Whitney. "How about you?"

"Excuse me?"

"What's got you so uneasy?"

Whitney didn't know what to say. "I don't—"

Grace held up one hand. "I didn't mean to spook you. It's just I get feelings, sort of like Wally."

"It seems like Wally's related to everyone in town. Don't tell me you and Wally are related."

"You got it. Wally's my distant cousin on my father's side."

"Wally really is related to everyone around here, isn't he?"

"Just about." Grace laughed. "I often thought Bliss should have been called Wallytown." She touched Whitney on the arm as she sobered. "You know, I think you should go out to the old burial grounds before you leave."

The hair prickled at the back of Whitney's neck. "Wally already suggested that."

"Then listen to him. Go and see it. You might find some answers."

"What sorts of answers?"

"I don't know. But I can feel that you need answers."

Whitney tried to smile, to pass off words that set her nerves on edge. "I'll keep that in mind."

Grace touched her shoulder. "Do that. Now let's talk about tents."

Whitney nodded, but before stepping into the tent she took one last look at Jake. He was standing now, alone, drinking something out of a bottle. She might be looking for answers, but Jake was looking for something more. And she understood right then what it was. Forgiveness and permission. Forgiveness for himself, for what he'd done, and permission to get on with his own life.

If Jake had known Whitney was coming along, he would never have agreed to come to the fairground to work. Just seeing her walk out of the hallway at the hotel, exposing his senses to her sleek beauty and delicate vulnerability, made him ache. For a tiny woman, her legs seemed incredibly long, and when her blue eyes met his he'd literally felt their impact.

He hadn't been able to stop to examine her throat, but he had been incredibly thankful that he hadn't been able to see any marks there. Then Emma had asked what had happened to her, and he'd seen the bruise on her shoulder, a round area of darkness against her clear skin, and reality had hit him in the gut.

She'd lied that she'd hit it on the door, and it sickened him that she'd had to cover for him. That's when he'd turned and walked out, needing distance, but not finding it when she'd come out and climbed into the van along with Emma.

During the drive, her voice had run over his frayed nerves, and he'd sensed her closeness with every breath he took. When they'd arrived at the fairground, he'd left her as soon as he could. And as he worked on the motor of the Ferris wheel, he'd tried to concentrate on what he was doing. But he couldn't stop tensing when he heard someone approaching, or stop glancing toward the tent where she was working.

Thankfully the lunches had been staggered and he'd sat down with cowboys and roustabouts, not Whitney. Around four o'clock, Wally came to stand by him, watching while Jake tried the engine that powered the ride. It cranked twice, then chugged to life and settled into a loud but constant rhythm.

Wally handed Jake a cold bottle of soda. "You need this," he said.

Jake cradled the cool dampness in his hands, then took a long, refreshing drink. "Thanks."

"Personally I think beer's better in the heat," Wally said.

"This is just fine."

"I told Les if anyone could make this bucket of bolts work, you could. And you did. You saved their skins, Jake, and I thank you for that."

"Don't thank me too soon," he said, pressing the half-full bottle against the inside of his wrist. "It's old and about worn out, and it's held together with spit and bailing wire. I think it'll work for now, but it's not going to last much longer."

"As long as it gets them through this holiday." Wally took off his Stetson and brushed at his face with the back of his forearm before setting the hat back in place. "Maybe they'll have enough money to have it overhauled after that, if their take's as good as it's been before."

"Did you find out about the part for my bike?"

He shook his head. "I've contacted everyone I know, but no one local's got it in stock. I put in an order with Carlson's, and the earliest they could get it would be the day after the holiday. I was hoping I could have it today for you."

So did he. "Thanks for trying."

"Wish I could have done more."

Jake turned off the motor for the Ferris wheel. "You can't get what you can't get." He looked around. "What else do you need me to do?"

"Well, Emma and me are staying out here with Les and Grace overnight. Maria's taking care of the hotel, and the garage is closed down tomorrow. What I need from you is to drive the van back for us. Whitney needs a ride and there's some things Emma set out for Maria to send out tomorrow with you."

The last thing he wanted was to be in the van with Whitney again. He downed the rest of the drink, then put the bottle down by the tools. "I can stick around here and help out some more."

"No need to," Wally said and held out a key ring. "Go ahead and take off."

Jake took the keys from the man and stared at them in his hand. "Why don't you just let Whitney drive it back?"

"Well, I could, but I was hoping you could do me another favor."

He looked up at Wally. "What's that?"

"You said you'd go back to the burial grounds before you left. I was thinking I'd really appreciate it if you'd take Whitney up there today before you go back to the hotel."

"Oh, no, I'm no tourist guide." He thrust the keys out to Wally. "You do it."

The man smiled, but shook his head. "Don't think I wouldn't like to. She's a nice girl, but Emma would have my hide if I took off now. Since you know how to get there, I thought it would be a good idea for you to do it."

When Wally didn't make a move to take the keys back, Jake shook them. "Wally, I'm not—"

"You still owe me two hours today. Consider it part of the job. Since you're still working for me for now, I'm asking you to help me out."

The old man knew how to hit below the belt. Jake closed his fingers around the key ring and drew it back. "This *wasn't* in the job description," he muttered.

"Neither was fixing a Ferris wheel," Wally countered wryly.

Jake pushed the keys in the pocket of his jeans, then reached for a rag and wiped at his hands. "All right, I'll go, but you can clean up here."

"No problem."

"Tell Les to prime the motor before he starts it. That might help to make it last longer."

"Sure will."

Jake tossed the rag on top of the toolbox, then looked at Wally. "See you tomorrow?"

"I'll be here."

Jake started to walk away, but Wally stopped him. "Jake?"

He turned to look at the old man. "What?"

"You're going to take a beautiful woman on a drive to a very special place. You could look a little pleased instead of looking like you're going to a funeral."

Jake shook his head. Under normal circumstances the man would be right, but not now, not with Whitney. "It is a burial ground, isn't it?"

"Good point," Wally said, then touched the brim of his hat. "Take care."

"See you," Jake said and walked away.

When he stepped through the entrance gates, he saw Whitney standing by the van. She looked remarkably fresh after a day with the temperatures in the high nineties, and in some way it annoyed him. Any normal woman would have been frazzled and worn out. Any normal woman would want to go back to the hotel, get a cool shower and collapse. Any normal woman would take one look at him and run.

But she didn't. She simply moved around to the passenger side of the van and got inside. As he got behind the wheel, she settled on the seat with a soft sigh. Out of the corner of his eyes, he saw her shift, rest her sandaled feet on the dash of the van, and the expanse of lightly tanned legs the action exposed seemed to taunt him.

Quickly he turned on the van, put it in gear and backed up, then swung around and headed out onto the highway. He kept his eyes on the road, not on her bare legs, but he found himself moving closer to the door and resting his arm on the warm metal.

"I'm really looking forward to seeing the burial grounds," she said as they headed toward Bliss.

He took whatever opening she gave him. "Why would you want to go out there? Believe me, there isn't much to see but crumbling rocks and heat and dust."

"Grace said I shouldn't miss it, and Wally made it sound pretty intriguing."

Jake gripped the steering wheel so tightly that his fingers ached. "It's like an oven out there," he said. "Why don't we just head back to the hotel, get something cold to drink and clean up?"

"We can do that later. Wally said that this is the best time of day to be there. He said the wind sings and the shadows move near twilight."

"I wonder what he smokes when he goes up there," he muttered.

"That's not fair." He cast her a slanted look and found her staring at him. "Let's stop playing this game."

"What game?" he asked.

"I know that you don't want to do this, but I do."

He turned back to the road ahead of them. "Look, it's hot and I've been working all day —"

"It *is* hot and *I've* been working all day, too. Did you know that every connection on a tent has to be wrapped and tied?" He could feel her still looking at him. "Or that the tents have special panels that have to be put in order or nothing works right? Or did you know that the dirt on the floor has to be raked absolutely level and that it takes two people to drill holes for the supports for the bleachers and fence ring?"

He held up one hand in surrender. "All right. You were working, too."

"Everyone was working."

"Of course they were. I know that." Bliss was in sight, and he knew he had to stop this madness now. "I think we should just scratch any idea of an excursion."

"Wally promised me you'd take me out there."

"He should have asked me first."

"Why? You work for him, don't you?"

"You know I do."

"The people that work for Les and Grace seem devoted to them. They've been with them since they bought out a wild-West show and carnival. That was twenty-four years ago. Since then, they've changed the wild-West show to a rodeo with local people participating. For eight months out of every year, Les and Grace tour the southwest with the show. When they're not working, they live in the motor home and they—"

He'd had enough. "What's wrong with you?"

"I don't—" she began, but he cut her off again.

"That's just it." He stared at the road ahead, the blacktop shimmering in the late-afternoon sun and Bliss not more than a mile ahead. "You *don't*. You don't know when to quit, when to run or when to get the hell out of my way!"

"Jake, all we're going to do is look at some burial place, then go to the hotel." She moved, taking her feet off the dash, and he knew she was turned toward him now. "I think you're really overreacting."

He would have laughed at the absurdity of what she just said if he hadn't been so angry. "Overreacting?"

"Don't you think you are?"

AN IMPORTANT MESSAGE FROM THE EDITORS OF SILHOUETTE®

Dear Reader,

Because you've chosen to read one of our fine romance novels, we'd like to say "thank you"! And, as a **special** way to thank you, we've selected <u>four more</u> of the <u>books</u> you love so well, **and** an Austrian Crystal Pendant to send you absolutely *FREE!*

Please enjoy them with our compliments...

Leslie Wainger

Senior Editor,
Silhouette Intimate Moments

P.S. And <u>because</u> we value our customers, we've attached something extra inside ...

EDITOR'S
FREE GIFT SEAL
THANK YOU

PEEL OFF SEAL AND PLACE INSIDE

HOW TO VALIDATE
YOUR
EDITOR'S FREE GIFT
"THANK YOU"

1. Peel off gift seal from front cover. Place it in space provided at right. This automatically entitles you to receive four free books and a lovely Austrian Crystal Pendant.

2. Send back this card and you'll get brand-new Silhouette Intimate Moments® novels. These books have a cover price of $3.50 each, but they are yours to keep absolutely free.

3. There's no catch. You're under no obligation to buy anything. We charge nothing—ZERO—for your first shipment. And you don't have to make any minimum number of purchases—not even one!

4. The fact is thousands of readers enjoy receiving books by mail from the Silhouette Reader Service™ months before they're available in stores. They like the convenience of home delivery and they love our discount prices!

5. We hope that after receiving your free books you'll want to remain a subscriber. But the choice is yours—to continue or cancel, anytime at all! So why not take us up on our invitation, with no risk of any kind. You'll be glad you did!

6. Don't forget to detach your FREE BOOKMARK. And remember...just for validating your Editor's Free Gift Offer, we'll send you FIVE MORE gifts, *ABSOLUTELY FREE!*

NOT ACTUAL SIZE

YOURS FREE!

*You'll look like a million dollars when you wear this lovely necklace! Its cobra-link chain is a generous 18" long, and the multi-faceted Austrian crystal sparkles like a diamond! It's yours **absolutely free** — when you accept our no-risk offer!*

THE EDITOR'S "THANK YOU" FREE GIFTS INCLUDE:

▶ Four BRAND-NEW romance novels
▶ An Austrian Crystal Pendant

PLACE
FREE GIFT
SEAL
HERE

YES! I have placed my Editor's "thank you" seal in the space provided above. Please send me 4 free books and an Austrian Crystal Pendant. I understand I am under no obligation to purchase any books, as explained on the back and on the opposite page.

245 CIS ANVV
(U-SIL-IM-06/94)

NAME

ADDRESS   APT.

CITY   STATE   ZIP

Thank you!

DETACH AND MAIL CARD TODAY!

THE SILHOUETTE READER SERVICE™: HERE'S HOW IT WORKS

Accepting free books places you under no obligation to buy anything. You may keep the books and gift and return the shipping statement marked "cancel". If you do not cancel, about a month later we will send you 6 additional novels, and bill you just $2.89 each plus 25¢ delivery and applicable sales tax, if any.* That's the complete price, and—compared to cover prices of $3.50 each—quite a bargain! You may cancel at any time, but if you choose to continue, every month we'll send you 6 more books, which you may either purchase at the discount price...or return at our expense and cancel your subscription.

*Terms and prices subject to change without notice. Sales tax applicable in N.Y.

He felt as if he was in a duel and he was unarmed.
"No."

"Well, you are."

He could see the hotel just up the street, and he
slowed as they neared the driveway entrance.

"We're going to the burial grounds, aren't we?" she
asked.

He looked at her. "What if I said we weren't?"

"You'd prove you were overreacting."

"Dammit," he muttered and went right past the
hotel. Silently he drove through Bliss and headed out
for the burial grounds.

Thankfully Whitney didn't gloat about him caving
in to her request. She settled into silence that lasted
until he was turning off the main highway and onto the
dirt road that led to the low hills across the desert
floor.

"Thank you for bringing me out here."

"Don't thank me," he muttered.

He put the van in a lower gear as the road started to
climb, and he could feel the motor laboring. Even the
van didn't want to be here. Just when he saw the heat
gauge start to rise, he drove over the crest of the road
and onto the mesa.

He saw Whitney sit forward, looking out the front
window at the mile-square area, and knew how spectacular the site looked as the sun began to go lower in
the sky. The sides, which climbed fifty feet straight up,
were sculpted by the light and shadows, with rich
browns and yellows layered in the strata.

Scrub trees and bushes were dotted through rocks
and drifted sand near the walls. The ring of rocks that
defined the outside of the actual burial area and the

two weathered pieces of wood on the view side cut sharp shadows on the dusty ground. A late-coming breeze teased the scrub brush, and near the edge of the precipice that overlooked the valley a lone tree stood like a sentinel.

Jake drove slowly across the uneven ground to a spot in the shade of a scrubby tree near the south wall, then stopped the van. "Well, here it is," he said.

Whitney opened the door and got out without a word, and as Jake came around to her she was staring out across the mesa. She rubbed at her arms with the flats of her hands and stood very still. "It's eerie, isn't it?" she asked softly.

It made him uneasy to be here with her just as much as the place itself made him uneasy. "I'd agree to that."

"There's something here." Her blue eyes were wide as they skimmed up the steep walls. "Don't you feel it?"

"You're spooked by Wally's stories. That's all." He was so close to her that he could have sworn he could feel her breathe. "Now that you've seen it, are you ready to leave?"

"Over there." She pointed toward the side of the wall that backed the area to the east and what looked like the remains of some sort of structure. He hadn't noticed it when he came by himself. "What's that?"

"I don't know, maybe the leftovers from the mining that was stopped."

She took off across the uneven ground, and he followed reluctantly. He'd just as soon be ahead so he wouldn't have a clear view of the curve of her hips and the stretch of her bare legs as she made her way to the wall. As she approached the adobe structure, little more than the crumbling foundation and rotting wood, he stopped.

He watched her touch the weathered clay, and when she drew back her hand he saw the dust from the blocks on her fingertips. Then she turned, her glasses in place, the dark lenses glinting back the late-day sun. "It's sort of like touching history," she said softly, rubbing her thumb over her forefinger.

"It's rotting adobe." He looked around the empty space, then back to Whitney. "Are you ready to go?"

"We just got here."

"This is it. What you see is what you get." He rocked forward on the balls of his feet. "Let's go."

"No. I want to see it all. It's incredible."

Nerves tightened his neck and shoulders. "In case you didn't notice, we're totally alone up here."

"Of course I noticed."

The wind stirred and he felt it brush the damp skin on his arms. "Lady, this place is isolated and godforsaken, and we're leaving." He tugged his cap a bit lower. "Now."

Her chin came up a fraction of an inch, and with slow deliberation Whitney took off her sunglasses. With the earpiece caught between her thumb and forefinger she swung them back and forth, the blueness of her gaze unblinking. She didn't say a thing.

When he couldn't stand it any longer he said, "What?"

She kept staring at him until he demanded, "All right, spit it out!"

She held out her sunglasses to him. "Why don't you take these to the van, then lock yourself inside while I look around. I'll make very sure we leave before dark, so you don't have to worry about turning into a were-wolf."

That was it. "Dammit," he bit out, wishing he could take her by her shoulders and shake some sense into her. But he knew how devastating it would be to touch her again for any reason. "This is *not* some joke!"

"Obviously," she said with all seriousness.

Jake exhaled with exasperation, deliberately look-ing at the bruise on her shoulder. "And you obvi-ously didn't hit your shoulder on the door."

She drew the glasses back and crossed her arms on her middle. "I could have."

"But you didn't. I hit you."

Just saying the words gave him an urgency to get out of here, but it didn't have the same effect on her. "You're not any more fair to yourself than you were to Wally before."

"What in the—"

"You were dreaming. That's not a federal of-fense."

As she cocked her head to one side, he saw the hint of a mark on her throat. His mouth went dry and he had to try twice to get out the next words. "God, I tried to strangle you." The words were low and hoarse.

She touched her throat with her hand, but her eyes held his. "Not deliberately. I wouldn't be out here with you if I believed you did." Her tongue touched her pale lips. "Jake, I'm not afraid of you."

Her words hung between them, and he wanted to grab them and hold them to him so they wouldn't dis-solve into nothingness, the way most things had in his life. But that was as impossible as this entire situation was. "Then you're crazy," he muttered roughly.

Whitney shook her head slowly, "No, I'm not. Neither are you."

He spun away from her and closed his eyes tightly. "You don't know a thing about me."

"I know enough to trust you," she said, her voice soft on the evening air.

He opened his eyes and stared blindly out across the mesa to the precipice to the west. The sun was turning blood-red as it touched the tops of the distant hills, and the breeze only brought air so hot Jake could barely feel it going into his lungs. "You can't trust me."

He felt her touch his back and the contact jolted him, sending a fear through him that seemed to rip at his soul. He spun around. "Don't do that!" His voice echoed off the walls and over the dusty ground. "Get the hell away from me." He fumbled in his pocket for the keys and thrust them toward her. "You take the van and leave."

She looked at the keys, then back to Jake, making him wish she still had on her dark glasses. "Not a chance. I'll be back after I look around," she said, then turned and started off in the opposite direction from the van.

He watched her go along the wall, her hands skimming over the rough rock, and for a moment he just stood there, feeling all control slipping out of his grasp. There was no way he should have brought her here, no way at all. It was too late to regret that, but not too late to put an end to it.

Then he knew it might be too late. He felt it coming, with each step she took away from him. Emptiness. Blackness. He was in a void, swallowed up by it, and he knew he was being pulled into "the hole." Curling his hands into fists, he pressed his nails into his palms, willing control. Fighting to stop it, but it didn't help.

Darkness. He was burning up, pain running through his body, but he fought being consumed by the murky horror of the hole. Not here. Not now. Not with Whitney close by. Not when he could get lost and strike out.

He tried to scream to warn Whitney, but all he could manage was a moan filled with despair. Worse, worse than it was. Hot. Burning up. Darkness. But when he knew the light would come to blind him, when the gun would be pressed against his temple, he was caught by the reality that he was on the mesa, at the ruins.

Miraculously it all stopped as abruptly as it had started. He was standing on the dusty ground, the sun was casting long shadows on the ground, and Whitney... He narrowed his eyes and scanned the area. At first he couldn't see her, then he caught movement and saw her at the curve where the wall jutted out toward the valley far below.

He had to get her out of here. *He* had to get out of here. "Whitney!" he called, but her name didn't come before she moved into the deep shadows in the wall. He blinked, but she was gone as if she had never been there.

The breeze died suddenly, and the stillness brought a heat that seemed to burn into his body, the way the isolation seemed to burn into his soul. He started running, going faster and faster. As his feet struck the sandy ground, he had the horrible idea that maybe he wasn't out of the nightmare at all. Maybe this was just a new one . . . with Whitney in it.

Chapter 8

Whitney hadn't looked back when she'd walked away from Jake. She hadn't trusted herself to look into his face again, to see his pain and be unable to ease it. Whether he believed her or not, she'd meant what she said. As the words came she knew that, no matter what, she did trust him. She couldn't let him push her away. She wouldn't.

As she picked her way along the rough ground, barely seeing what she passed, she tried to think of what to do next. She felt helpless, weighed down by the lies she'd woven around the two of them since she'd agreed to Cutter's scheme. Yet she knew that telling Jake the truth wasn't even a viable option right now.

By the time she reached a sweeping curve in the wall that angled it back toward the precipice, her clothes were clinging to her and she could feel moisture trickling down between her shoulder blades. She looked ahead and saw an opening cut in the rock-and-clay wall, supported and shored up by heavy timbers wedged into the rough, a seven-foot-high hole that had to be part of the old mining scheme.

She went closer and stopped by a ridge of drifting silt that had built an irregular barrier about five inches high at the threshold. At first there was nothing but blackness inside, then her eyes adjusted and she could see a mine tunnel. The ceiling was supported by heavy beams that crisscrossed overhead, and massive timber pillars were spaced along the inside walls.

She took a step closer, and right then whatever breeze there had been was gone. The heat grew, becoming so oppressive that she felt light-headed. Maybe she should have gone back to the hotel with Jake when he insisted earlier. The heat was making her feel sick. As the idea of going back to Jake grew, a sudden coolness came to her, a faint whisper of a breeze that sang over the uneven surface of the tunnel interior. It touched her skin, easing her discomfort and pushing away the heat.

She had no idea what could cause it in this place, but she didn't hesitate stepping over the silty threshold and going into the shadows ahead. She inhaled the cool air, relishing the odd freshness that touched it. Intrigued, she took a couple more steps, and the cool air stirred gently around her, teasing her hair and brushing her skin.

She stared ahead, barely able to make out the tunnel wending off to the right into inky blackness. She started to go farther, but was stopped by Jake calling her name.

"Whitney!"

His voice echoed back and forth in the tunnel, surrounding her in an oddly complete way, as if it came from every direction at the same time. And as she turned, she saw him silhouetted at the entrance, the setting sun at his back, splashing reds and purples across the sky.

"Whitney?" he gasped as he took off his sunglasses.

"I'm in here."

Jake lunged into the mine, stumbling over the silty ledge. He lurched to the left, righted himself and came toward her, one hand held out into the darkness as if to ward off what he might find there.

Instinctively she put out her hand to touch his and for a moment their hands met. His heat pressed against hers, then his fingers tangled with hers and he pulled her toward him.

She looked up at him, the dim light hiding definition, but she didn't need to see clearly to know something had happened. His breathing was labored and ragged, and the coolness all around only accented the burning heat that seemed to radiate from his body.

"Jake?" He heard Whitney's voice surrounding him. "Jake, what's wrong?"

She was there, right in front of him, "in the hole." God, he'd pulled her into it with him. He'd brought her into nightmares and horror. Black. No air. Buried. It hadn't ended, just grew hideously perverted, drawing Whitney into it.

He jerked his hand back, freeing her, his only hope that she would slip out of the nightmare's hold if he didn't touch her. But that hope was dashed when he heard her speaking, so close to him that he thought he could feel her heart beating beside him. "Jake, please, tell me what's happening?"

"Die now!"

The cold of gunmetal at his head.

And he knew a need to kill was a living thing in him. His hands shot out, ready to squeeze the life out of the one who was going to kill him.

No, it was Whitney. He knew that. She was here. And he remembered last night with her over him, his hands at her throat, her eyes filled with fear.

"No!" he screamed. The sound torn from the depths of his soul to explode into the darkness. "No!" He knew right then that he'd end his own life before he'd hurt Whitney again.

He found the strength to move, to jerk back, and he stumbled against the wall, splinters of wood pressing into his back. Run. That was all he could do. Run. He lurched to his left, then saw the light and went for it. Stumbling over the uneven ground, he broke out of "the hole," into deep-red light. Like blood. Everywhere.

He faltered, then realized he was caught in the last rays of the setting sun. Drawing air into his tight chest, he looked ahead. The burial grounds. The desert. This world. He knew he was back.

"Jake?"

Whitney's voice was right behind him, but he didn't turn. He couldn't. He had to run, and run like hell. But when he tried to take a step, his legs gave out and he dropped to his knees. The rock and sand pressed into the palms of his hands as he hit the ground, and he knew a truth that cut him to the bone. He couldn't outrun the visions, not any more than he could outrun the wind.

All he could do was make sure that Whitney was safe from the demons that he knew were going to destroy him.

Whitney stood in the entrance to the mine, so shaken that she had to hold on to the wooden post for support. Jake was not more than five feet from her, on his knees on the ground and his hands pressed into the dust and rocks. His hat was gone, hair falling forward partially veiling his face, and his ragged breathing was the only sound she heard.

She had to try twice before she could get a single word past the tightness in her throat. "Jake?"

He was motionless for a long moment, then he slowly stood, steadying himself with his hand on the wall by him, as if his legs had lost the ability to hold him up. He exhaled in a rush, then finally looked at her. "What in the hell were you doing in there?" he demanded roughly.

"It was cool, and I was just looking. I didn't know it would cause so much..." She lost the word she wanted.

He ran a hand over his face. "Well, it did."

"You shouldn't have gone in there."

"Thanks. I think that's pretty obvious," he muttered. "I thought you had claustrophobia?"

"No, not really."

His expression tightened. "You said—"

"That I knew what it felt like. I've known people with it."

"Now you know one more," he muttered. "It's time to get the hell out of here."

He drew back his supporting hand from the wall, then with a swipe at his jeans he walked away from her and toward the van.

She wished she could stop him and make him tell her what happened to him when he sank into the terrors that threatened to consume him. But as long as he could walk away and drive off, there was no hope of that. He'd escaped from the terrorists and saved his life, but he'd never stopped trying to escape since then. He tried to escape from his old life, from everyone he knew, and from getting help.

She hurried after him, only catching up to him when he stooped to pick up his baseball cap near the ruins of the building she'd looked at first. He hit the cap across his thigh to get the dust off, then put it on. He pulled it low over his face and kept going toward the van, his long legs quickly eating up the distance.

He was already in the van and behind the wheel by the time Whitney got there and scrambled in on the passenger side. Before she'd even closed her door, she knew something else was wrong. Jake was turning the key, but the motor wasn't cranking. All that happened was a series of hollow clicks. Then the clicks began to die until there wasn't any sound at all.

Jake hit the steering wheel with the flat of his hand, then opened the door and got out. He went around the front, jerked up the hood and disappeared from view as he leaned in to work on the motor.

Whitney sat alone in the van for several minutes, sorting through what had happened. And it began to blend with the last time she saw Fillerman. She closed her eyes to fight the feelings of helplessness and frustration that came so easily when she remembered.

Fillerman had closed down, briefly answering questions that were safe. But when she asked for any details of his time with his captors, he'd been vague and uncertain. She could still remember when he'd walked out of the office the last time.

"You don't understand. I don't have any answers for you."

She'd tried so hard to reach him. *"All you have to do is remember."*

He'd turned ashen at her words. *"That's just it. If I remember, I'll die."*

"Whitney!"

She was startled by Jake yelling at her, and she looked up to see him peering at her around the side of the car hood. "I'm sorry. What?"

"Get behind the wheel and, when I tell you to, turn the key over. Then we'll get the hell out of here."

She could feel his nervousness, the need to escape, and for a moment Whitney wondered if in some strange way she'd been granted a wish. If the van didn't work, Jake couldn't leave. If he couldn't leave, he had to stay with her for a while longer.

"Are you ready?" Jake called out to her.

She scrambled over to the driver's seat, touched the key and yelled. "Ready."

"Turn the key!"

When she did the clicking was stronger, but the engine didn't crank at all. She stopped, but Jake called out to her again, "Keep turning it."

She did and the clicking got weaker and weaker.

"Hold it," he said, then, "Try again."

She did what he asked, but nothing happened this time.

His oath was loud enough for Whitney to hear it clearly, and she got out of the van to go around to the front. Jake was leaning into the engine compartment doing something with wires near the back. Without looking at her, he said, "See if you can find a flashlight in the van."

Whitney looked through the van, and in the back she found two wrenches, a screwdriver, a quart bottle of water and folded blankets pushed under the back seat. But no flashlight. Picking up the tools, she went back to Jake. "No flashlight, but there's blankets, some bottled water and these."

He glanced back over his shoulder and frowned at the meager assembly of tools she held out to him. "If I can't see, I can't use the tools."

"What about the headlights?"

"They won't light up the engine," he muttered and kept working.

"Then we're stuck."

He didn't acknowledge her statement but kept working even though the engine compartment was so dark Whitney was sure he couldn't see much.

"Jake, come on. Stop. You can't see a thing, and the van's not going anywhere."

He kept fiddling with the wiring, and Whitney finally stepped back. There was nothing she could say to make him stop and nothing she could do to make anything better. She looked away, and she realized night was here, with its subdued heat, the buzz of insects and a huge full moon just clearing the crest of the ridge behind the burial grounds.

It was huge and orange, streaked with wispy clouds, and looked like an enormous ball someone had hung in the velvety night sky. It looked so close that if she stood on tiptoes, she could reach up and touch it. But she knew that was as much a fantasy as her thinking she could reach Jake, that she could do something, anything, to help him or Cutter.

Jake slammed the hood of the van so hard she swore she felt the ground shake under her feet from the impact. When she looked back, Jake was staring at her, his eyes dark and shadowy, and for a heart-stopping moment she thought he was lost again. She wasn't sure she could endure seeing him go through that one more time and being terrified that he wouldn't come back.

"We need to get out of here," he said, and she knew he was here, not in some dark part of his past.

"How? Emma said this is eight or ten miles from Bliss. I don't know about you, but I'm not walking that far."

"What do you suggest?" he asked.

"That we stay until someone comes looking for us."

"Wally and Emma won't even know we aren't there until tomorrow some time when we don't show up at the rodeo."

"Then we'll have to wait until morning."

"Oh, no, we won't," Jake said.

"All right. Any other suggestions?"

He scuffed at the ground with his boot, stirring the dust. "Yeah, you take the van. I'll stay out here."

"Excuse me. I'm *not* staying in the van. It would be like trying to sleep in an oven." She tugged at her top, freeing the clinging cotton from her damp skin. "It's hot enough out here."

The light from the full moon crested over the rise, and its pale glow robbed everything of color. The world became black, gray and white, and Jake's eyes were the blackest of blacks. "Then I'll take the van and you sleep out here," he said.

She held up one hand. "Oh, no. I'm not staying out here alone with overfriendly snakes."

"Lady, in case you haven't been paying attention, you've just run out of choices."

"No, I haven't. Emma's got some blankets in the back. We can lay them out and—"

He took off his cap and slapped it against his thigh. "Like hell *we* can."

She flinched, but didn't back down. "I don't care if you lay out the blankets ten feet apart, I just don't want to be out here alone."

He tucked his hat in his back pocket, then grabbed the tools out of her hand and went to the back of the van. A moment later he came back with the blankets under his arm and the bottle of water in his hand. He put the bottle on the bumper of the van, then held out one of the blankets to Whitney.

"Put it wherever you want to put it, and if you see a snake, yell."

She took the blanket and held it to her breasts. "Where are you going to put yours?"

"Anywhere you aren't putting yours," he said bluntly and walked away from her.

She'd let herself believe that the van breaking down could have been a blessing, but Jake was doing his best to make sure she wasn't any closer to him than she would have been back at the hotel in their separate rooms.

Jake tossed his hat through the open window of the van, then he headed toward the burial area. Dust kicked up under his boots as his long legs put more distance between them. She grabbed the bottle of water and hurried after him. "What do you think's wrong with the van?" she asked as she caught up with him.

"Your guess is as good as mine," he said without stopping as he circled the rock perimeter of the burial area.

"My guess isn't worth two cents, actually. I don't know a thing about cars." She slowed to get her footing on the rough ground, and Jake got ahead of her. "You're the mechanic," she called as she tried to catch up.

"My diagnosis is it won't start."

"*Why* won't it start?"

"It isn't getting any power, and I've done all I can do without tools or testing equipment." When he stopped abruptly, she barely kept from running into his back. Then he turned and the moonlight did nothing to hide the anger in his expression. "Would you stop doing that?"

"Doing what?" She was standing so close to him that she had to tip her head back to look into his face.

"Following me."

"I...I wasn't. I mean, I was looking for a good place to settle."

He swept one hand toward the area behind them, and she realized she'd followed Jake to the corner of the grounds, to where the high walls at the southwest broke away for the drop-off that overlooked the valley below. "Take your choice. It's all yours."

The land was bathed in moonlight, the rocks and wood pieces starkly pale in contrast to the long, dark shadows they cast. "I'll put my blanket wherever you put yours."

"Lady, what do I have to do to make you face reality?"

Reality? She looked up at him and could feel his close presence so intensely that it was making her heartbeat race. Reality was Jake only had to be close, to look at her, and she started to feel like some teenager with raging hormones. That was stupid. What she felt around this man hardly qualified as sophomoric.

The strength of the emotions he could evoke in her made her take a half step back, something to stop the feeling of extra heat where his body was close to hers. And it minimized the sense of size and maleness that he seemed to radiate, even when he was so annoyed with her that she knew he'd love to shake her until her teeth rattled.

She wasn't about to put a name to those feelings, not here, not now. She swallowed, needing a drink of the water, but not at all certain she could even open the bottle right now. "Do you think you've got a corner on reality?"

He shook his head. "I seem to have a corner on putting you through hell, and I won't set you up for that again."

She knew who had been going through hell, and it wasn't her, not by a long shot. But she didn't want to debate that with him right now. "Okay, I'll make you a deal." She hugged the blanket and bottle of water to her. "Give me the van keys, and let me sleep three feet from you. If anything happens, I'll run and lock myself in the van." He hesitated. "That's my best offer," she said.

He shook his head. "The keys are in the van," he said and turned from her to walk to where the soaring wall ended as the land fell away. He shook out his blanket, then dropped down and sat with his back against the granite wall. With one leg stretched out in front of him, and the other bent, he rested his forearm on his knee and stared out across the desert below.

Whitney moved closer to him, then spread her blanket in front of a large rock on ground that looked fairly smooth. Then she sank down on the heavy cotton fabric facing the view and crossed her legs Indian style. She opened the water bottle, took a long drink of the warm liquid, then asked, "Do you want a drink?"

"No."

"Are you sure?"

"Uh-uh."

"Is that a yes or no?"

He turned, and the moon that was climbing higher in the sky cast his eyes in such deep shadows that they couldn't be read. "It's a no."

Cradling the bottle in her hands, she turned from Jake and looked off into the distance. The full moon bathed the land in its light, turning the distant hills into mere suggestions of shadows against the horizon. As a star shot through the heavens, a mournful howl echoed in the night, and Whitney felt her skin prickle.

Wally believed there was more here than dust and stone and wood. And as she sat there she felt a niggling sense of something . . . but she couldn't begin to figure out what that "something" was. She wondered if that was what set Jake off in the mine, if he'd sensed something that drove him into the darkness that he carried in his memories.

She looked back at him—his head resting against the wall, his face turned from her and his hair partially obscuring his profile. His hand on his thigh was closed in a fist, and she knew he wasn't sleeping.

As another howl broke the night, Whitney said, "Jake?"

"Yeah?"

"What was that?"

"A coyote."

"It sounds close."

"Close enough."

She darted a look back at the burial grounds, the two pieces of wood at the entrance blurred in the moonlight. And they looked like guards, protecting the site. "Do you suppose the coyotes might come down here?"

He turned, his eyes as dark as the night itself. "They won't."

"How can you be so sure?"

"They don't want to be around us any more than we want to be around them."

"I still don't think I'll be able to sleep."

The option was definitely one she was considering. "You can't stay up all night."

"Why not? I've done it before. Of course, not in the middle of nowhere, with goodness knows what creeping around." She rubbed at her arms. "It's not exactly like being in California, camping on the streets in Pasadena to make sure you get a good view of the Rose Parade on Christmas Day."

"No, it's definitely not like that," he said in a low voice.

His file said Jake had lived in Malibu, a beach town near Los Angeles until he walked out on everything. His beach house, an expensive car and hand-tailored suits were locked up, and a bank account that was impressive hadn't been touched. The man near her was a far cry from the man who had lived the good life before. "You've been in California?"

"A long time ago."

"Did you live there?"

"I was there." He shrugged. "Now get some sleep."

"How about you? You've been working hard all day."

"I don't plan on sleeping. It's not exactly my friend."

"Insomnia?"

"Oh, I can go to sleep, but I won't."

"You can't just sit there all night."

"It's either that, or taking a chance. You know what happens when I sleep." The rough sound of laughter was there for a second, but without any humor in it. "Hell, you know what happens when I'm not sleeping."

She didn't move, afraid to in case he just stopped talking again. "No, I don't know."

"Lady, you were in my room last night. Just look in a mirror at the marks on your neck and shoulder. You were in the mine up here. That's what happens."

"But what causes it?"

He rested his head back against the wall and exhaled harshly. "I don't know. Sleeping, being awake, getting in tight places, feeling trapped, a smell, a person. The list is endless.''

"It just happens?"

"I can be sitting at a desk, reading, drinking coffee and the next thing I know they're there."

"Who's there?" she asked softly.

He made a dismissive movement with his hand. "Things. Images. Crazy, demented visions. I live them. I'm in them. They take over." He stood abruptly and turned his back on Whitney as he went toward the drop-off. He stopped at the very edge, pushed his hands into the pockets of his jeans and rocked back and forth, the ground crunching under the heels of his worn boots. His shoulders hunched forward protectively, and his head was down.

"What started it?" she asked.

She saw him exhale on a shudder. "There was an incident about a year ago. I had some trouble."

"When you killed that man?"

"That was at the end of it, I thought." He kept rocking back and forth. "But it never stopped, not really."

"You said he was going to kill you. Why?"

He shook his head. "Actually, it was nothing personal. I was just in the wrong place at the wrong time?"

"Where were you?"

"On the other side of the world."

"What happened?"

He stilled. "Man's inhumanity to man."

She sensed his need to talk, yet he held back, keeping the past at bay. Worse, she didn't know how to get him to look at it and tell her what he saw. "In what way?" she finally asked.

And a question thrown in because she didn't know what else to ask found the chink in his defenses. "Locking a human being up in a space that is little more than a coffin, with dirt for the floor and walls, filled with the stench of sewers and so hot you don't know if you're breathing, except for the smells, always the smells. Never moving you, always the same place, living in your own filth."

As he started rocking again, his shadow from the moonlight came toward her, almost falling on her knees, then it drew away, then came back. She had the idea if she put out her hand she could touch it, but that was as foolish as believing she could listen to his words without pain. She pressed her hands to her thighs and kept silent as he spoke in a low, strained voice.

"There's no light anywhere, just darkness, until he opens the door. It blinds you. He forces you to your knees, puts a gun to your head and pulls the trigger on an empty chamber. And the laugh, it's like some demented hyena. If you fight, or even if you flinch, he makes you lay on your face in the filth and beats you."

She swallowed hard, tears burning her eyes as she closed them.

"So you stay awake, forcing yourself to keep your eyes open. They burn and hurt, but you don't sleep. You think of ways to escape, to get out. You listen, you try to find a weakness. But you don't. You just take what he gives, and you take it until you know he is going to kill you. It's over. He doesn't need you anymore.

"So you strike out, you get a hold on him, and you beat on him and you kill him. You stop him. You make a break for it. You get lucky. You run and run and run, and finally you're free."

She heard him moving, and when she opened her eyes she saw Jake sitting down on the edge of the drop-off. His back was to her, his hands pressed to the ground on either side of him.

"Then the final joke with a huge, cosmic punch line hits you." He was silent, then whispered, "You aren't free at all. You just take it with you. The darkness, the suffocation, the terrors. You tuck them in your mind and you can't push them out."

She got to her feet, her legs weak and unsteady. His words struck at her soul. If she could, she would have taken his pain. She went to him, but forced herself not to touch him. Silently she sank down beside him, leaving space between them and letting her legs hang over the edge as she looked at him.

He was staring off into the distance, his eyes narrowed, his jaw set. "They come out when they want to, like they did last night. Like they did in the mine. I can't stop them." He looked right at her, and the bleak weariness in his face broke her heart. "I can't."

"So you stay away from people, and you keep moving, and you wait for it to all happen again?"

"Sometimes you drink until you black out, and you make sure that you're never too close to anyone. You never let anyone care about you."

She was stunned by the sudden thought that he couldn't stop her from caring about him. As that idea sank in, she knew it was even more than that. She *did* care, but she knew she could care even more, care with a single-mindedness for this man that could take her breath away. And it wouldn't stop at caring.

"Or you stay out in the open and you don't sleep," he said.

"You can only do that for so long," she murmured.

He sat motionless, the night surrounding them, then abruptly he got to his feet and looked down at her. "You look as if you've seen a ghost."

The only ghosts she'd seen tonight were Jake's, and now it was hard enough just looking at the man. "I was just thinking about everything you said."

"I told you those things to make you understand how important it is for you to keep your distance from me."

"And you keep your distance from everyone."

"I do what I need to do, not what I want to do."

She got to her feet to face him. "If you could do whatever you wanted to do, if this never happened, and things were right, what would you do?"

He tucked his hair behind his ears, then pushed the tips of his fingers in his pockets of his jeans with a sharp, jabbing motion. "Right now, if I could do what I wanted to do..." His voice trailed off into the night around them, but his gaze lingered on her lips.

Chapter 9

"What would you do?" Whitney breathed.

Jake looked down at her. The words he'd been terrified to say out loud for so long had been said. He'd told her things he thought he could forget forever, and he was still here. He wasn't lost in the dark, drawn into the past. Now she wanted to know what he wanted to do.

Cautiously he reached out, and against his better judgment he touched her. He framed her face with his hands, the moonlight making her skin look like alabaster. What he truly wanted was her, to have a life where he could take her here and now. But as he looked into her eyes, he saw forever in there, not one night.

He didn't have forever to offer her. If he had her once, he'd never stop. He'd never be able to let her go and walk away. His thumb played along her cheekbone, and he felt her tremble under his touch. He'd told her so much, exposed a part of his soul to her that no one had seen before, under the guise of trying to make her understand why he couldn't be this close to her.

"Jake?" Her tongue darted out to touch her parted lips. "What would you do?"

Her skin felt like silk under his touch, something so beautiful against the ugliness that had become his life, that he lost direction. He should have let her go, made her keep her distance, used words or force, whatever it took. But instead he leaned toward her, then slanted his mouth over hers. The taste of her that had lingered in his mind was in his mouth again, and all he could think of was fate had just one more cosmic joke up its sleeve for him.

Beauty and gentleness and sweetness. And he had it under his hands. Yet touching Whitney, he knew he could destroy her just as easy as not, and it was a risk he didn't want to take. A risk he knew he couldn't take. Yet as her mouth yielded to him, as her arms went around his neck and her hips pressed against his, desire, a pure emotion born from fire, encompassed him. And his need for Whitney was so fierce that it blocked out everything else.

If this place was the field of ghosts, it was also a place where anything could happen, where anything he wanted could be his.

He felt her sink her fingers into his hair, tangling with it, then she arched her head back and her gaze met his. A fire as hot as the one in him flared in the depths of her eyes, and his response to her only deepened.

And as her hands skimmed over him, leaving a trail of fire as they came to rest on the thin cotton of his T-shirt, he knew she felt his arousal. He felt as if he'd burst from his need. The war inside him was devastating. This couldn't happen, yet it was the most needful thing he'd ever experienced. He was terrified of what could happen if he loved her, and he was terrified what would happen if he didn't.

In a desperate attempt to end this before it got entirely out of hand, he lowered his hands to her shoulders. To push her away, he told himself, but as she shifted and tugged his T-shirt free of his jeans, he froze. The cotton was loose, and her hands worked their way to his bare skin. He gasped as her fingers trailed up to his nipples, and he tried one more time. This time with words.

"This is all wrong."

"It feels right," she whispered as she pushed the cotton up, then pressed her lips to his chest.

He trembled, and he knew this was it. Either stop it or be damned. His hand moved. He was going to pull her hands off him, but instead he found himself touching her. Through the thin material of her top, he felt her heat, then the weight of her breast cupping in his palms. And any will he had to do the sensible thing was crushed.

He felt her swell and her nipples harden under his touch, then her hands were moving lower on him to tug at his belt. "Whitney." Her name was a low groan in the night air, and when she pressed her hand to the denim stretched by his desire a madness took over.

He grabbed her, cupping her bottom with his hands and he lifted her. As light as a feather to him, she cir-

cled his neck with her arms, and her legs wrapped
around his hips. As her head arched back, making
their contact so intimate that nothing was hidden from
him, he touched his lips to her neck. The pulse in the
hollow of her throat beat frantically against him.

He gave in to his needs, an ache that had been
growing in him since he saw her by the side of the road
in the light from the setting sun. Since he'd looked into
those amazing blue eyes, felt her skin under his hands,
and tasted her mouth with his. As she clung to him,
her lips nibbling at his ear and his jawline, he held
more tightly to her and began to rock. Even though
their clothes were still a barrier between them, the
contact sent jolts of pleasure through him that defied
description.

Her fingers dug into his shoulders, and she gasped,
"Yes, Jake, oh, yes."

Somehow they'd made it to her blanket, but Jake
had no memory of carrying her there. He lowered her
to the cotton, never losing the contact between them,
and when she was under him, her hands grasped his
shirt, tugging at it, frantic to have the material gone.

He moved back, stripped off his T-shirt and tossed
it behind him. Her hands spread on his bare skin,
branding him with her heat. And he wanted to feel her
the same way. Gently he pulled up her shirt and she
helped him get it over her head, then he threw it in the
general direction of his shirt.

In the moonlight, he saw her breasts, barely con-
cealed by a flimsy excuse for a bra. His hand trembled as he pushed the fine material aside and allowed
his hands to feel what had only been hinted at through
her top. Her breasts weren't large, but full and ele-

gant. "You're beautiful," he whispered as he lowered his head to take her nipple in his mouth.

Just then the blare of a car horn ripped through the fabric of the night, and the sound ripped Jake back to reality. He jerked back to look over the rock and saw headlights beyond the burial grounds in the vicinity of the van. He looked back down at Whitney and she was gazing up at him. Her eyes were heavy with desire, her exposed breasts swelling, and there wasn't an ounce of embarrassment in her expression.

He could have taken her here. He *would* have taken her here. But as reality thudded securely into place when the car horn sounded again, he knew how close he'd come to doing more damage than he'd ever done in his life.

What he wanted from this woman went beyond desire, beyond lust. He pushed himself away and fumbled for their shirts. It could go into realms that he'd never entered before. It could have gotten to the point where he could love her. His hand crushed the shirts as he grabbed them, and he was thankful he wasn't looking at Whitney anymore.

He turned, tossed her shirt toward her and slipped his on over his head. Tugging it down, he stood, knowing that there was no hiding the way she had affected him. "The rescue squad," he muttered. "I'll go head them off."

And he walked away from Whitney. One part of him was thankful for the reprieve, the other part fought an agony that he knew could consume him. He went toward the lights, and he raised his hand to shield his eyes so he could see past the brilliance. Wally. The man stood by an old pickup, his hand in the driver's window, no doubt on the horn.

"Here!" Jake yelled. "We're here!"

Whitney adjusted her clothes, then sat on the blanket, sensing the lights behind her, but not about to turn. She raked her fingers through her short hair and tried to breath evenly. She'd never dreamed she was capable of such uninhibited passion. That she could be with a man and blot out everything else in the world. It had never happened to her before, and under the best of circumstances, she would have been hard put to understand it. Right now she was in shock.

"Whitney!" She heard Jake calling to her. "Whitney, it's Wally."

She stumbled to her feet, her blanket and the water bottle in hand. Crossing to Jake's spot, she got his blanket, then bunching them in her arms she turned and saw the headlights. Heading toward them, she tried to center herself. What happened, happened. That was it. She had wanted it to happen. She could have stopped it. She knew she could have. She knew Jake was just waiting for her to do that very thing. But she hadn't.

She trudged over the uneven ground, skirting the burial grounds, and went closer to the lights. She'd wanted Jake to make love to her. She'd wanted him to love her. That thought was staggering. To love her. That meant she could love him. She felt chilled, despite the balmy night air. She knew she was so close to loving this man that the line she had to cross to love him barely existed anymore. It was hard to be that honest with herself.

Honest? The chill grew. About the only honesty she'd had with Jake was with her body. Everything since Cutter had arranged for her to be here with him had been lies. And she hated that. She looked ahead, able to make out Wally and Jake standing by a beat-up old pickup truck. Honesty. It had to come. And it had to come soon. No matter what.

"Wally decided to take a drive up here," Jake said as she approached. "Lucky for us."

"Yes, lucky," she murmured and looked at Wally. She hoped against hope that the man's intuitive powers weren't working overtime tonight. "You came to visit the ghosts?"

"I came to sit and listen," Wally said. "I guess you two had a lot of time to sit and listen."

"I think it takes a person like you to do that," Jake said and moved away toward the van. "How about putting your lights over here so we can see about this?"

"Sure." Wally got into the pickup and maneuvered it until the headlights were on the engine compartment of the van. He left the truck idling and got out to cross to the van. "What's the problem with this old buggy?"

"No power," Jake said, trying to get the hood up. "It doesn't crank at all."

"That's strange. Just put a new battery in it a few months back with an alternator. And the starter's only a year old."

"Try it and see for yourself," Jake said as he finally got the hood up.

Whitney crossed to the passenger side as Wally went around to get in behind the wheel. Through the window, she saw the old man turn the key. The engine cranked once, then started.

"No problem," Wally said as he got out. "I guess she's just temperamental."

Jake closed the hood and pressed both hands flat on the metal. "I don't believe it."

Neither did Whitney. Then she remembered the coolness in the mine, and her wish that the van couldn't take Jake away from her. Foolish ideas, she knew, but for a moment in time she wondered if there was something up here, something that knew what each person who came here needed. If the van had started, Jake would never have stayed, he never would have told her about his nightmares and he never would have touched her the way he had.

She realized Wally was talking to her, and she had to regroup. "I'm sorry. What?"

"I was just telling Jake that strange things happen up here, things don't always have a rational explanation."

"More hocus-pocus talk?" Jake muttered.

"No. I'm just saying that there wasn't any reason for the van to not start."

"How about a loose wire or a corroded connection?"

"Sure. And how about the van doesn't start so you can sit up here and listen for a while?"

"Hell, if *they* wanted that, all they had to do is ask," Jake muttered.

Wally grinned at that. "Maybe this is how they asked."

"I give up," Jake said. "Are you coming back to the hotel, or staying here to talk to your friends?"

"I told you, I'm here to listen. I'm staying here for a while, then I'll head back to the fairground. I just need to—" he grinned "—get my battery charged."

Jake shook his head, then went around and got in the van while Wally came to Whitney. "So what did you find up here?"

An answer came out of nowhere, and it made her heart skip. She'd found a man in pain, a man who touched her soul in a deft way that went well beyond physical attraction. She found a man she could love. "I don't know," she said, then got into the van. As she put the blankets and bottle of water on the floor between the seats, Wally swung the door shut.

She turned and he was holding on to the window frame with both hands. "You'll figure it all out sooner or later, little lady."

"I guess so." Then she remembered the mine. "Have you been in the old mine shaft on the other side?"

"Sure have."

She didn't know how to say this without sounding a bit foolish, but she made herself ask the question. "Was there a coolness in it?"

His shaggy brows drew together. "In the mine?"

"Yes."

"It's been like an oven when I've been in there. Why?"

"Nothing," she said.

He looked past Whitney to Jake who was tugging his baseball cap on over his long hair. "It was cool in the mine?"

Jake shook his head. "I don't know. I wasn't in it very long."

Wally shrugged. "How about you go by the station in the morning and make sure everything's all right and locked up tight. Then come on out with Whitney when you can."

"I won't be coming," Jake said.

"You gotta bring Whitney out."

"She can take the van."

"I need you to keep an eye on the Ferris wheel. Besides, you need to have some fun, son. It's part of the job. The rodeo's going all day, and the carnival opens at noon. But the night's the best time." He slapped the door with one hand and stood back. "See you both. Now get on back and get some rest."

Jake slipped the van in gear, drove around the old pickup, then headed away from the burial grounds. When they hit the highway and smooth road, Whitney glanced at Jake. He drove in silence, without a trace of the nearly explosive closeness they'd experienced minutes ago.

She could have almost thought she'd hallucinated, or that the ghosts had played tricks on her. But she knew the ache deep inside that refused to completely go away was real, and she knew if she touched her tongue to her lips, she'd find his taste lingering there.

Turning from him, she stared out the window at the night and the desert, then she saw the faint glow ahead from Bliss.

"Whitney?" Jake said, finally breaking the silence.

She turned to look at him in the shadowy interior of the van. The low glow from the dash lights cast eerie shadows across his face and showed the tension in his jaw.

"Yes?"

"That was all my fault back there."

"Your fault?" Her voice was little more than a whisper. "I wasn't exactly fighting it myself."

He cast her a sharp look. "Listen to me, things almost got out of hand. I could have taken you there and then. To hell with reality. To hell with sanity. Thank God Wally showed up."

"If he hadn't?"

The hotel was in sight, its light spilling out into the night. As Jake swung onto the driveway and headed for the entrance, he said roughly, "You know damn well what would have happened."

She couldn't think of anything she'd wanted more in her life than to lie with Jake, to feel him by her and over her, to have him love her. "Would that have been so terrible?"

He hit the brakes harder than he had to, and the tires caught at the gravel, stopping the van with a forward jerk. But Jake didn't get out. He turned to Whitney, shadows doing little to hide the intensity in his expression. "When I was locked up, when I sat in that filthy hole for hours and days and weeks and months in the dark, surrounded by *filth*, I kept my sanity by visualizing a normal day."

"I don't—"

"You know, keep normal by dreaming normal. And I did. I dreamed of getting up, eating breakfast, going to work, then to a business lunch, back to work, then I went to dinner, to some great restaurant. I went home, had a drink, did some work, then went to bed. And do you know what?"

She shook her head, words caught in her throat.

"I had beautiful women, one after the other, waiting for me."

She knew her face must be red, and the idea of him being with a woman, even in his imagination, was off-putting to her. "What does—"

"When I escaped and got back to my so-called normal life, I did the same things, in the same order, except for the last one. I went to bed alone. There wasn't anyone in my bed. I didn't want anyone with me."

"Why not?"

"Because I wasn't fit to have anyone that close. I was seeing a woman before it all happened. She was an attorney at my company. We seemed to understand each other, until all hell broke loose in my life. Six months later when I got back, we didn't connect at all. One day I looked up, and she was gone. I was relieved."

"Why?"

His hand gripped the wheel so tightly that she could have sworn she could see paleness in his knuckles. "Because no one else belonged in my life. No one had a part in the ugliness. Not then, not now." He paused. "Especially not you."

She could feel the sting of tears behind her eyes, and she hated the idea of crying in front of him. Especially when the tears weren't from pain but from frustration. She'd come so close to touching him, to finding the reality of the man, and now it was a solid concrete wall again. "You can't tell me what to do or what to feel."

"If I gave you any idea back there that there could be something . . . anything between us, I'm sorry."

"Oh, you're sorry?" she muttered. "Thanks, but sorry isn't good enough. And sorry won't change things. God, I'm sorry that you're in pain. I'm sorry that you cut yourself off from everything and everybody, and I'm sorry that I care."

She didn't wait for him to respond before she tugged the door open and got out. Hurrying around the back of the van, she headed for the porch steps and almost got there before Jake had her by her arm. He pulled her around to face him, and the light from the hotel shone on his face.

His expression was filled with anger and pain. "Don't care," he bit out.

"You're too late, way too late."

He flinched as if she'd hit him, then slowly let her go, breaking the contact between them. "Go on. Go to bed."

She didn't move.

"Whitney, go to bed." There was a raw desperation in his tone as he repeated himself.

She knew desperation herself. But she knew she couldn't do a thing about it right now. She was tired of fighting for every inch of progress with this man, then have him pull away. Weariness made her legs feel weak, and a vague headache was beginning behind her eyes.

She lifted her hand, not caring that she was trembling. Although Jake flinched at the contact, she touched his chin with the tips of her fingers. She felt the bristling of a new beard under her fingertips and the tension in his jaw. "You don't go to bed alone anymore, do you?"

He frowned at her. "What are you talking about?"

"You don't even go to bed. You sleep outside or on the floor by the doors. You can't even get into the bed in that room."

He covered her hand with his and pulled it away from his face. His fingers were tight on her, hovering this side of pain. "Why are you doing this?"

"No matter where you sleep, you sleep alone," she whispered and pulled her hand out of his. Without looking at him again, she turned and went up the stairs into the hotel.

Whitney went through the empty lobby, down the hall, into her room and closed the door. She made it to the bed before her legs gave out, and she sank down, letting herself fall back on the spread. Staring at the ceiling, she couldn't get the look on Jake's face out of her mind. Why had she said that? Why had she struck out at him when all she really wanted was to hold him and not let go?

The ring of the phone startled her, and she pushed herself up to grab the receiver before it rang again. Her nerves couldn't take the shrill tone again. "Yes?"

"Miss Tate," a woman with a slight accent said. "This is Maria. I thought I heard you come in."

"I just got back."

"A man is calling for you."

She didn't want to talk to Cutter right now. "Could you tell him I'm asleep?"

"He has called before...several times. I do not know if he—"

"Never mind. Go ahead and put him through."

There was a double click, then the line was open. "Hello?"

"Where have you been?" Cutter demanded in a rushed voice that only made Whitney feel more on edge than before.

She glanced at the bedside clock and was shocked to see there were still fifteen minutes before it was midnight. It seemed as if they had been up at the burial grounds for an eternity. "I was out for a while."

"At least you're there now. Have you got anything for me?"

She closed her eyes. "No."

"Nothing?"

"He's been talking, but he's not specific. There aren't any details or even the names of any locations." She heard Cutter exhale over the line. "What's been happening on your end?"

"There's a report that the terrorists are planning something in the next couple of days. I wondered if they'd do it on the Fourth. Whatever it is, it's not good."

Whitney knew all about the ways those people used to prove a point or to prod along negotiations. "You haven't had any luck tracing him?"

"None. You'd think with them moving him all the time, they would have left some evidence somewhere."

Then she knew. "They aren't moving him."

"What's that?"

"From what Jake's told me, they didn't move him at all. They kept him in some hole and he didn't leave it until he broke out."

"One place? What did he say about it?"

"He said it was really small, not much bigger than a coffin, and it had dirt on the floor and up the walls, and it was totally dark. I don't think he could hear anything, other than what they let him hear. And one man was the only contact he had. That's the man he killed when he escaped."

"Anything else?"

"It stunk. He kept mentioning the smell."

"What kind of smell?"

"A sewer. I think he said it smelled like a sewer, and it was really hot."

"Was there anything else at all?"

"A bright light when they opened it up, but any light would have been bright after complete darkness."

"He didn't mention anything about a village or town or—"

"No, nothing like that."

"Okay. Do your best to get something specific as fast as you can. Something about the location, where he broke out, where he went when he got out, if he talked to anyone getting to the embassy."

"I'll try," she murmured.

"Stay close to him."

She lay back down on the bed and closed her eyes. "Cutter, he mentioned a woman he was seeing before he was abducted. Maybe she'd know something you could use."

"Forget that. We contacted her and she doesn't know a thing. When he got back, he didn't talk about it at all with her, and she finally stopped seeing him. She said she was tired of feeling as if she was invisible, that he never touched her after he came back."

She rested her forearm over her eyes. "So she left him?"

"From what she told me, he drove her away."

She wondered how any woman could have turned her back on Jake and left him to his demons. If she cared, he couldn't have made her stop. "Then she's no help at all?"

"None."

Whitney was startled by a door opening, then closing nearby. "I'll . . . I'll call you tomorrow," she said as she slowly sat up and stared at the wall that her room shared with Jake's. "Goodbye."

She fumbled to put the receiver back on the cradle without taking her eyes off the wall, and she waited. A minute later, she heard a muffled thud, then the patio doors next door being opened. Jake was in his room.

Something in her relaxed. He hadn't taken off. He was still here. She stood and stripped off her clothes, then went into the bathroom and started the shower. When she stepped inside, she welcomed the comfort of the warm water on her bare skin.

Then quietly tears came. And as the water surrounded her, she cried for Jake, for what he went through, for his pain and his loneliness. And she cried for herself because she was trapped between truth and lies, between Jake and Cutter.

Chapter 10

It wasn't nightmares that haunted Jake that night. It was Whitney. Her words followed him into his room as he opened the patio doors and turned and saw the unused bed in the shadows. She was right. He'd never slept in it. And he knew he wouldn't begin sleeping in it tonight.

He started to turn, but for an instant his eyes seemed to played a cruel trick on him. In the shadows, it almost looked as if someone was in the bed. And even though he knew he was totally alone, he thought he saw Whitney, desire filling her eyes the way it had at the ruins. If he moved, would she be there for him, would her bare skin look like fine porcelain, would her breasts swell under his touch?

"You're plain crazy," he muttered to himself as he shook his head sharply and reached for his bedroll.

There wasn't a woman in his bed, much less Whitney, and he'd make very sure she never would be there. He shook out the bedroll on the tiles by the open doors, then stripped off his clothes and headed for the bathroom. But even a shower didn't clear away the memories.

When he finally stretched out on the bedroll in his briefs, he looked up at the sky, trying not to let his mind drift back to what had happened at the burial grounds. But it was impossible not to remember. Even if he didn't let the images fill his mind, or if he made himself not relive the moment when he felt her under him, his body remembered.

Frustration was a living thing for him, and he almost got up and left to walk out into the emptiness of the desert. But he made himself stay where he was, knowing just because he left physically, he couldn't leave the remembrance.

When sleep began to tug at him, he fought it, afraid there would be nightmares born out of the words he'd said to Whitney. But as the grayness crept up on him, the suggestions of dreams were blurs of reality, with the only recognizable occupant being Whitney.

Whitney looking at him, reaching out, touching him. Whitney laying under him, naked, inviting him to take her. His hands on her breasts, on the sleek lines of her stomach, then... He awoke with a start, his skin damp and his breathing rough. He wasn't surprised that just a dream about the woman could bring him to full arousal.

He lay very still, willing his body to relax, to let go of the need that ached in him. He concentrated on breathing, on making his mind blank, but nothing worked. As soon as he closed his eyes, she came to him in the misty shadows of his mind, so tempting, so beautiful.

And he finally gave up. He didn't fight it anymore. With a low moan, he rolled onto his side. At least he could have her now in dreams that weren't night-mares any longer.

July 4

When Whitney woke, the sun was high in the sky, and she could tell from the shimmering of the air out-side that it was already hot. With a glance at the clock, she was surprised that she'd slept until just after eleven. She rolled out of bed and dressed quickly in denim shorts, a white tank top and strap sandals. Without bothering to put on makeup, she ran a brush through her hair, then went out onto the patio and looked over the low wall into Jake's room.

She exhaled a breath she hadn't been aware she was holding when she saw his bedroll was laying in a tan-gled heap by the open doors. Jake was still in Bliss. She went back into her room, then out into the hall and down to the lobby.

She found Maria, a tiny woman, barely five feet tall, with long ebony hair that fell halfway down her back, wearing a bright red full shift, sweeping the tiles near the front doors. She looked up at Whitney and smiled. "Good morning, miss, it is a nice day for a holiday. No?"

"Yes, it is," Whitney said. "Have you seen Mr. Hill around?"

"He left early this morning."

Whitney crossed to the entry and looked outside. When she saw the van was gone, she turned and closed the door. "Did he go to the garage?"

Her head bobbed. "Oh, *si,* that is where he went."

"Did he say when he'll be back?"

"No. Did you want something to eat—lunch or a late breakfast?"

"Yes. Maybe a sandwich, some fruit and something cold, maybe iced tea?"

"Right away," Maria said and hurried out of the lobby into the kitchen.

Whitney crossed to one of the small tables at the back of the room where she could see the doors clearly and sank down in a wooden chair. Either she stayed here and waited for Jake to come back, or she walked into town to the garage.

She glanced at the wall clock by the doors and decided if Jake wasn't back at the hotel by one o'clock, she'd head into town to find him.

At five minutes to one, the entry door opened, and Whitney looked up from the magazine she'd been reading to see Jake walk into the hotel lobby. In his tight jeans, the plain white T-shirt, cowboy boots and that ever-present baseball cap, he made her mouth go dry and her heart race.

She knew then she would never be able to look at him in the same way again. She'd never be able to look at him without remembering how close she'd come to really knowing him. Or how close she had come to falling in love with him.

She pushed away the magazine she'd bought her first morning in town and deliberately turned the cover down so the face of the ambassador wasn't visible. Pressing her hand on the smooth coolness of the paper, it didn't do anything to stop the heat that was rising in her. Control yourself, she insisted mentally, fighting her basic response to the mere sight of the man.

She made herself stand slowly, and when Jake spotted her she tried not to react to the harsh frown that tugged his eyebrows together over his dark eyes.

"I was wondering when you'd get back," she said.

"You've been waiting?"

"I don't have any other way of getting out to the rodeo. That is, if the van's still running."

He slipped off his hat and snapped it against his thigh, an action she knew came when he was tense or angry. His dark hair was pulled back in a low pony-tail, setting off the harsh angles of his face. "It's running just fine, thanks."

She went toward him, stopping at the edge of the carpeted area. "I was wondering, after last night. That was kind of spooky, the way it wouldn't start for anything, then it started right up when Wally tried."

"Wally told you it's temperamental."

"As long as it's going now, that means you can take me out to the rodeo."

He put his hat back on and pulled the bill low over his eyes. "It's well over one hundred degrees out there, and it's not my idea of fun to bake in the heat while some cowboy ropes a calf. Maybe when it cools off, I'll run you out there."

"I don't mind the heat. They've got shade set up and lots of fresh lemonade."

"Well, I hate lemonade, and I *do* mind the heat."

She stood her ground. "Wally wanted you to take a look at the Ferris wheel again. Why not take me out there, check the Ferris wheel, then come on back here? You don't have to stay if you don't want to."

"Whatever." He took his sunglasses out of his back pocket and slipped them on, and all she could see now was her own reflection staring back at her in the lenses. "Let's get this over with," he muttered.

Maria came up behind Whitney. "Miss?" Whitney turned and Maria was holding her magazine out to her, the picture of the ambassador fully visible to Jake. "You left this."

Whitney grabbed the magazine and rolled it up as she turned back to Jake. With his eyes hidden, she didn't have a clue if he'd seen the front of the magazine. Clutching it tightly in her hand, she said, "Let's go," and moved past Jake for the door.

Whitney had expected a good amount of people at the rodeo and carnival site, but she hadn't expected to find the parking area all around the chain-link enclosure filled with cars and trucks and horse trailers. The informal parking lanes spread out in all directions, and people were making their way to the entry gates in a steady stream to get their tickets.

From the road, she could see the rides in full swing, and a huge balloon that looked like a cowboy floated high in the air over the fun house. As Jake drove off the highway onto a single lane outlined by ropes and posts, Whitney could hear raucous country music mingling with the clamor of engines, laughter and shrieks of delight. A cowboy handed them a parking ticket through the window, then directed them to the right toward the outside perimeter.

Jake drove slowly through dust being stirred by the cars in front of them, and a blaring announcement for the "Ten-and-under barrel racing," boomed over the speakers, drowning out the other sounds for a moment. A light breeze stirred the hot air, bringing the odors of livestock and hay mingling with popcorn, into the van.

"Who would have thought there were enough people within a hundred miles of here to pack this place?" Jake muttered as he inched his way along.

"They sure didn't come from Bliss." She leaned forward to get a better look at everything. Through the fence, Whitney could see throngs of people milling around, carrying balloons, eating cotton candy and carrying huge stuffed animals. "Have you ever seen anything like this with the dust and crowds and all the excitement?"

"A few times."

"You've been to carnivals like this?"

"The same type."

"Where were they?"

"I don't remember the places. I just remember working there."

"You *worked* at carnivals?"

"I had a strong back and a need for money at the time, and they needed someone to do the dirty work."

"I guess I assumed you went when you were a child, that your mother and father might have taken you?"

"They died when I was five."

She hadn't had any idea that he'd been that young. Cutter's notes had only said, "parents deceased—only child."

"I'm sorry. I didn't realize—"

"Don't be. I don't really remember them at all."

"Who raised you?"

"Anyone who signed up for the foster family program." He swung left and headed up an aisle that went toward the fences at the back. "I was in a lot of foster homes."

"Didn't you have any other family?"

He eased the van through a tight space where a car had parked too far out in the aisle, then he flexed his fingers on the steering wheel. "No one showed up to claim me."

"I'm sorry."

"Don't do that."

"What?"

"Don't feel sorry for me. I don't need it. I don't want it. I survived. I've always survived."

Yes, he had survived, but Whitney wondered what the cost had been for that survival? Before she could say anything else, he said, "I'll swing back around to the front and let you out. Tell Wally I'll come back later and see about the Ferris wheel when I can get a parking space."

She knew what he really wanted to do, to let her out and drive off, and she wished there was some way to stop him. Then the answer to her wish appeared ahead of them near a cluster of storage sheds that backed up to the carnival area.

Wally. He was scanning the crowds, wearing a new-looking black Stetson, polished black boots and a

turquoise shirt worn with black pants. When he spotted the van, he waved and motioned to a space roped
off near a service entrance by the sheds. He hurried to
undo the ropes, and he stood back to let Jake pull the
van into the space.

When the van stopped, Whitney didn't get out. She
waited to see what Jake was going to do. Wally came
up to the driver's door and looked in the van. "I was
getting ready to head into town and find out what was
keeping you two."

"Jake didn't get back from the garage until just a
while ago," Whitney said as slipped on her sunglasses.

Wally glanced at Jake. "Any problems?"

"No, I was just doing some clean up on her car so I
can get it going as soon as the parts show tomorrow.
I'm going to go back and take the heads out of the so-
lution now."

"That can wait," Wally said. "The motor on the
Ferris wheel's squealing like a stuck pig. I don't know
what's wrong with it."

"I told you it wasn't going to last."

"I know. I know. But Les is stressing out over it,
and if there's a chance of fixing it to keep it going until tonight, I know you're the one who can do it."

With a shrug, Jake turned off the van. "I guess I
can take a look at it."

When Wally stepped back and opened the door for
Jake, Whitney got out on her side and went around
the front of the van. Wally started for the service gate.
"Come on. They're waiting."

Whitney followed Wally past a guard at the gate and
onto the carnival grounds. As Jake came in after her,

she looked around at the booths that lined the way, at the balloons that floated in the air. The shouts of booth workers trying to get people to try their games blared all around.

Wally touched Whitney on the shoulder. "We're heading over to the Ferris wheel. Why don't you look around for a while? The rodeo's pretty packed right now, but later on the crowds should thin out. Don't miss the baking booths, but steer clear of the fortune teller."

"Why?"

"She's new, her and her brothers, and if she's psychic I'm a pig's ear." He grinned at her. "Just have a good time, and we'll see you later on."

She nodded and watched Wally and Jake head off until the crowd swallowed them up and she couldn't see them anymore. Looking over the crowds, she could see the huge Ferris wheel sitting still, the cars on the wheel moving slightly in the hot breeze.

Whitney moved back into the shade of the nearest booth and almost jumped out of her skin when someone shouted, "How about trying your hand at winning a teddy bear, pretty lady?"

She turned and saw a blond kid dressed like a bandit holding out a handful of white balls to her. "Hit the bull's-eye, dunk the sheriff and choose your prize."

A portly man in a white jumpsuit was sitting on a swing suspended above a huge tank of water behind the kid. From the looks of him, he'd been dunked several times, and in this heat he probably welcomed it. She shook her head. "No, thanks."

As she turned to leave, she almost walked into Emma. The woman's hair was hidden under a cowboy hat, and a loose top and jeans were already dotted with moisture. "Hey, I thought it was you!" Emma said. "How do you like all this?"

"It's incredible."

"Wait until tonight. Then you'll really see something. How about something cool to drink?"

"That sounds wonderful."

Whitney fell in step with Emma as they went through the milling crowds. "Wally tells me that the two of you got stranded up at the burial grounds."

"The van wouldn't start."

Emma stopped in front of a concession stand and spoke to a flushed-looking girl behind the counter. "Roxy, two big lemonades."

While the girl poured them, Whitney looked at Emma. "You said you've been up there quite a few times, didn't you?"

"I've spent a lot of time up there over the years. When I was a kid it was a favorite make-out place. Not the burial place itself. Even kids know you don't set foot in there. But the rest of it..." She smiled. "You know, deserted, isolated. A terrific view. I got to really know Wally up there, actually."

Whitney knew she was blushing at the images that Emma's confession conjured up for her. Making out? It had been much more than that. "I know Wally's the one who thinks things up there are...different, but haven't you ever thought that?"

"Honestly, I probably have. I just downplay it because Wally's so vocal about it." Emma turned to take two huge cups from the concession girl, then handed one to Whitney. She didn't speak until they were walking again, heading off toward the side of the arena. "What do you think you found up there?" she asked.

Whitney took a long, cool drink of the lemonade, trying to think of what to say. Then she finally just said the truth. "I'm not really sure."

Emma stopped and looked past Whitney, then said, "Let's go someplace where we can talk, honey."

People jostled Whitney as they passed by. "I don't think such a place exists around here right now."

"You're in luck. I know the owners," Emma said and lead the way.

Whitney followed her through the crowds, then off to the right and to the motor home parked behind a series of booths that were displaying baked goods. Emma stepped up and went inside, then Whitney went in after her.

The interior was cool from a small air conditioner humming in the window, and when Emma closed the door the noises outside were muffled. She motioned Whitney to sit at a small table by a window that overlooked the midway. As Whitney sank down on the vinyl bench, she smoothed the damp exterior of her drink with her fingers.

"All right," Emma said settling opposite her. "What do you think you found?"

She took a sip of her drink before she spoke. "Have you been in the mine shaft that's up there?"

"Sure. Why?"

"When we were there, I went in. It was boiling hot outside. It was cool in the mine. Not just cooler, but really cool. It felt almost like air conditioning." She laughed a bit nervously. "I know that sounds crazy."

"Maybe. Did Jake feel it, too?"

She shook her head. "No, he doesn't like closed-in places. He was only in it for a minute. Did Wally tell you about the van?"

"He mentioned it wouldn't start."

"It was running fine when we went up there, then suddenly it wouldn't start. I mean, Jake did everything he could think of to it, and it was dead. We had to stay. Then Wally showed up hours later and it turned right over."

Emma sat back. "What are you saying?"

"I don't know. It's all so farfetched, but I was wishing that Jake couldn't just run off. There were things I . . . we needed to talk about, and he was going to leave."

"And the van wouldn't start?"

"Yes."

It felt good to say that to someone, to get it out, even though she knew it sounded incredibly weird. But Emma wasn't laughing. She actually looked as if she was considering what Whitney said, as if it had been the most rational thing in the world. The woman took a drink of lemonade, then looked at Whitney.

"You think something kept you there?"

"It sounds crazy, doesn't it?"

"I've heard of stranger claims about happenings up there than a car that won't start. Although what would be the point of the cave being cool?"

Whitney suddenly knew why. "I wouldn't have gone in it if it hadn't been cool, and Jake wouldn't have come after me."

"Why did you want him to come after you?"

"I didn't. I mean, I didn't plan it. But something happened that..." She couldn't believe she was talking about "things" happening as if it was all rational. "There's probably some logical reason for the coolness, maybe an air vent or something, and maybe the van just was too hot to start."

"You might be right," Emma murmured.

Whitney glanced out the window, and in the middle of the press of the people on the midway she spotted Jake immediately. He was walking with Wally, his cap shading his face, and they were heading for the motor home.

She kept her eyes on Jake as he made his way through the crowds. Wally said something that struck Jake funny, and when he laughed Whitney quickly looked away. The expression transformed Jake, literally making him years younger, and in some odd way making Whitney wish she was the one who had brought the smile to his face.

"Whitney?"

She looked at the woman. "I'm sorry, did you ask me something?"

"I was wondering what you're doing in Bliss? This isn't exactly on the map of tourism for Arizona."

Whitney had a strange notion that Emma would see through any story she came up with, so she didn't even repeat the vacation lie. "I'm working, actually."

She glanced out the window and Jake was gone. The crowds moved and shifted, but Jake wasn't anywhere in sight, and she had the sinking feeling that he was probably on his way back to the hotel.

"I didn't think you were on vacation, but how on earth could work bring you here?"

Whitney sank back on the bench seat. "If I tell you something, can I count on you to keep it to yourself, that you won't even tell it to Wally?"

"That's hard. Wally and I don't keep secrets, but since this doesn't have anything to do with him, I can assure you it won't go any further."

And Whitney told Emma the full truth. The woman listened in silence, asking nothing until Whitney finished with her coming to find Jake in Bliss.

"No wonder he seems so . . . so lost."

Whitney flinched mentally at her words, but knew they were true. "He's lucky to be alive. He's the only person we know of who escaped from those terrorists."

"So you need him to tell you what he remembers from the time they had him?"

"I really need some clues about the place where they kept him. We think the ambassador's being kept there."

Emma sat back. "Tell him the truth. I would."

Whitney shook her head. "I wish I could, but I can't. He'd run. He's done it before."

"But he's never known you before. You might be surprised if you opened up to him."

"And if he doesn't, the ambassador can't be helped." She rotated the almost empty cup between her palms. "I can't take that chance."

"No, of course you can't. This Cutter person, the man that's been calling you, he's put you in a terrible situation."

"Terrible" hardly covered the way she felt about the lies and the pressure. The door opened right then, and Wally stepped up into the motor home. His face was flushed, and he tugged off his Stetson before wiping at his forehead with his forearm.

"What's going on, Wally?" Emma asked.

"That's what I'd like to know." Wally came over and dropped down in a chair by his wife. "Jake's all set to head back into town, and the van's dead. It won't start. It won't even turn over. I've checked out everything. So has Jake, and we can't find a thing wrong with it."

"Just like it did last night at the burial grounds?" Whitney asked.

"That's what Jake says. Whatever it is, looks as if he's going to have to hang around until the guy who borrowed the pickup gets back or until he can hitch a ride with someone going back to town."

Emma looked at Whitney. "It seems Jake can't just take off. Our van's being temperamental."

"Yes, it does." Whitney stood and asked Wally, "Where's Jake now?"

He shrugged. "He's plenty frustrated. The last I saw of him he was going toward the rodeo arena."

Whitney wasn't going to question what happened with the van, she was just going to take advantage of it. "I'll see you both later," she said and headed for the door.

Jake stood in the heat at the rodeo arena, leaning against a bleacher support as he watched a kid trying to rope a skittish calf. The boy lost his hat right out of the gate, but eventually got his lasso around the animal's neck, and the crowd cheered.

Jake jumped when a hand touched his shoulder, then someone spoke to him. "I thought you hated watching calf roping while you're baking in the heat."

When Jake glanced to his right, he was looking into a face partially hidden behind oversize sunglasses. But that didn't hide the smile on her pale pink lips or the effect that expression had on him.

"I thought I did, too," he said. "But I don't have a choice for a while."

"What's going on?"

"The van's dead . . . again. The pickup Wally borrowed last night is gone. Some kid took it into town and hasn't come back. So I'm stuck."

The crowd's cheering drowned out everything for a moment, then it quieted down enough for him to hear Whitney ask, "Did you get the Ferris wheel going?"

"For now."

"What are you going to do until you get a ride back to town?"

He shrugged. "I guess I'll stand in the heat and watch some cowboy rope a calf."

"How about testing the Ferris wheel?"

He looked down at her. "What?"

"You fixed it. You need to test-ride it."

He'd resolved to keep his distance from Whitney and that didn't include riding on a Ferris wheel with her. "That's hardly necessary."

Unexpectedly she took his hand, her fingers curling around his, and he was taken aback that the touch felt easy and as natural as anything he'd ever experienced. "Then come and look around the carnival with me. I've never been to one."

His immediate reaction was to put much-needed distance between the two of them. He wasn't going to put her in jeopardy, not again. Then he realized they were outside in a huge crowd. There weren't any mines, or any burial grounds, or any way they'd be isolated.

And the idea that this might be a gift came to him, a time when he could be with her, see her smile and feel her hand in his, and she wouldn't be in danger from him. A break in the woven threads of reality. It sounded possible to him, and just a bit desperate.

"Come on," she said. "It's better than standing in the heat watching calves get caught, isn't it?"

As she smiled up at him, and her hold on his hand tightened, he threw caution to the hot desert wind. "All right. But just until I can leave."

"Just until you can leave," she said with a smile.

Chapter 11

By the time the sun was beginning to set, Jake was walking with Whitney down the crowded midway and facing the magnitude of his mistake. Far from being a gift, the past few hours with Whitney had bordered on torture. He couldn't be close to her without wanting to touch her, and when she brushed against him from time to time, he knew one touch wasn't enough.

He didn't have to work at remembering the feel of her holding him, her legs around his hips, her lips against his skin. The memory was just there, a part of him that he didn't know how to rid himself of. Now if he just looked at her, at the dampness of her hair clinging at her temples, or at the sleek sheen to her skin, it set thoughts racing through his mind that no amount of sour lemonade or rides on rickety Ferris wheels could blot out.

As the colored lights that were draped overhead from booth to booth began to flash on, Jake knew it was time to end this farce. "It's time for me to get going. Wally should have the van going by now, or the truck'll be back."

"And if the van still doesn't work or if the truck isn't back?"

"It's only a few miles. It's cooling off. I'll walk or hitchhike back."

"I'll come with you."

He stopped and glanced at her, the twinkling lights reflecting in her eyes and her lips lifting in a smile. Right then, her image hit him as hard as any fist he'd ever taken in the stomach.

"No." He heard the biting abruptness in his response and he regretted it when he saw her expression falter. "Listen, I just meant that it's time for me to get out of here. Stay and enjoy yourself. Go on the Ferris wheel again, or eat more cotton candy. Go and see some calves roped. There's no reason for you to leave, too."

She tossed her drink into a garbage container by the fortune teller's booth, then turned to Jake. "Where are you going to go?"

"Back to the hotel."

"Why?" she asked, tugging at her top to free the damp material from her skin.

The action reminded Jake of the first time he saw her by the side of the road next to her dead car. The effect on him hadn't changed. It had only grown in intensity, and as the material settled to cling to her breasts he muttered, "I'm tired and hot." And he wasn't going to push his luck being around her any longer.

He looked away from her, hoping to kill the responses she could draw so easily from him. But as he glanced to his right, he froze. In the shadows not touched by the overhead lights of the midway, he saw his past. As paralyzing panic filled him, Jake knew he had gone totally mad and he'd been too late leaving Whitney.

This time there was no blackness, no fading into a place of torment. He was in the middle of hundreds of people, facing the man who had tortured him. The man who had laughed while the pain made Jake scream. The man who Jake had murdered.

He felt people moving around him. He heard the music, the voices over the loudspeakers, the screams of delight from the games. No darkness, no searing red, no distorted visions. Just the man standing by the fortune teller's booth not more than ten feet away, dark and swarthy, with black hair slicked back from a face dominated by a hawkish nose and gaunt cheeks.

He wasn't real. He couldn't be. He had to be Jake's own personal nightmare. But when he moved out of the shadows, Jake braced himself, ready to kill again. His hands ached with the need to stop it, to make it end once and for all, then suddenly everything changed.

Under the lights of the midway, Jake realized there was no scar on the man's cheek, or the hard edge to his features. Hair that had been as black as night had streaks of gray in it, and the body under loose black clothes was stocky, not wiry.

God, it wasn't him. It was all a horrible mistake. He'd been fooled by the shadows and fooled by his own mind. The man stood right in front of him now. "Want your fortune told?" he asked, a twang in his voice as he motioned to the fortune teller's booth. "Madame Saleena knows all and tells all."

Jake shook his head, his mouth still dry from the fear of moments ago. He'd almost lost it, right in the middle of the midway with hundreds of people all around. No place was safe for him.

"Ah, come on. I saw you out here, trying to work up the nerve to do it," the man said. "Like the sign says, look into your future for a dollar."

Jake didn't want to look into any future he might have. He didn't need some fortune teller to know that there was no Whitney Tate in that future. "No, thanks."

The man shrugged and looked past Jake at Whitney. "How about you? Do you want Madame Saleena to look into your future?"

Jake saw Whitney as she shook her head. "No, thanks."

As the man shrugged and walked off to approach another couple nearby, Whitney looked at Jake. But there wasn't anything in her expression except a touch of impatience. "Can you believe that act? Madame Saleena knows all! And that's her brother trying to get business for her."

A degree of thankfulness filled Jake. He'd thought the episode with the stranger had taken forever, but it must have happened in a few moments. He obviously hadn't done or said anything out of the ordinary. Whitney didn't have any idea what had just happened to him, or he knew she wouldn't have have let him get away without talking about it.

"I'm going to find Wally." His voice sounded fairly normal and his relief grew. All he had to do was walk away. Just leave and find Wally, then get out of here.

But as he turned from Whitney to go, there was a piercing whistle, then the world turned white with bright light. Jake flinched as the light blinded him, and the terror stabbed at him again. Then explosions were everywhere, the acrid smell of gunpowder filling his nostrils. Blue and red lights flooded over him, another thundering explosion seemed to rock his body, screams were all around and he knew it was all over.

Whitney watched Jake as he started to leave her in the middle of the midway, and as the firework display began Jake froze. People were shouting and clapping as fountains of color exploded in the sky overhead and firecrackers filled the air with sharp retorts.

But one look at Jake, and Whitney knew he was seeing something entirely different. His eyes stared heavenward, his complexion ashen in the showers of brilliance, and his skin was filmed with moisture. With each explosion, he flinched, his arms rigid at his side, his jaw clenched.

She had to get him out of here. The fireworks splashed their colors over the heavens, building up to the grand finale. She knew Jake would never survive that.

"Damn you, Cutter," she muttered under her breath, then chanced touching Jake on the arm.

His skin was sleek with dampness, and she could feel his muscles trembling, but he didn't react to her touch at all. His eyes stared upward, and his breathing was rapid and harsh. "Jake?" she said as close to his ear as she could get. "Jake, it's me, Whitney. Let's go."

When she tried to urge him forward by pressing at the small of his back with her other hand, he uttered an expletive that shook her and suddenly lunged forward. Before Whitney could do anything, he'd run into the sea of people who were cheering and yelling for each spectacular display and disappeared.

She went after him, trying to push through the crowd, but feeling as if she were trying to run in mud. When she finally broke free, she was at the side entrance where she'd first entered the carnival with Wally and Jake. She looked around frantically, but Jake wasn't anywhere in sight.

Then she knew the one place he'd head to for his escape. She ran over to the guard by the gate. "Did a tall man in jeans and wearing a ball cap just go out here?"

"Yeah, he did."

"Thanks." She pushed open the gate and stepped out into the dusty parking area. She headed to where the van was parked, and even before she was close enough to see into the shadowy interior, she knew Jake was there. She could hear the rapid clicking sound of the key being turned and his rough voice chanting an obscenity over and over again.

As she got closer, she could finally see Jake clearly. His hand gripped the top of the steering wheel and his forehead was pressed to it as he tried over and over again to start the engine. She hurried around to the passenger door, and as she grabbed the handle she

found herself praying that the van would start. It was
a matter of life and death for Jake to get out of here.

She braced herself, then jerked the door open and
scrambled into the van. As she sank down on the seat,
Jake turned on her.

"Get the hell out of here!" His face was distorted.
"For God's sake, leave me alone!"

She held tightly to the cold metal of the door handle, ready to run if she had to, but knowing she
wouldn't. "I'm coming with you."

With a curse filled with desperation, he sat back, his
head against the seat, and his ragged breathing echoed in the van's interior. "Please," he finally whispered hoarsely. "Go away."

The fireworks were almost over, the grand finale
filling the skies with brilliant beauty, but all Whitney
saw was the spray of exploding colors playing across
Jake's face. Her heart literally hurt to look at him, to
see the desperation and the pain there. "I want to
help," she said.

He flinched when an explosion outside almost
shook the van. "No one can help me."

"Jake, that's wrong. There's help. I swear there is."

The noise outside seemed to die away as Jake
growled, "Do you know what that son of a bitch used
to do to me? He'd come into 'the hole,' into this filthy,
stinking hole in the ground, and he'd put the gun to
my head. He'd tell me to get ready to die. Then he'd
pull the trigger on an empty chamber and laugh hys-
terically when I'd scream." His voice was low and
shaky, touched by an aching pain that shook Whitney
to the core.

"That gave him some perverted pleasure, some sense of power. And when he couldn't get me to scream that way, he made me scream any way he could." He exhaled harshly, and she saw his hands lying open on his thighs, palms up, almost as if in surrender. "He was remarkably inventive. Then he found out that noise was as painful as silence. I'd go days without any sound at all, feeling as if I'd been buried alive, yelling and screaming just to hear my own voice.

"Then he'd fill the hole with noise, with recordings of explosions and screams and machinery and traffic, all together in a horrible, grating mixture. He'd play it for hours, for days, until I was screaming again."

She didn't realize she was crying until she felt a tear splash on her hand, but she didn't wipe at the moisture. She never took her eyes off Jake as hatred for the man who had done this to him surmounted every emotion she'd felt for another human being, except the love she felt for Jake.

Love. Her eyes trailed over his tense profile. Yes, love. So simple. And it hadn't come with stars and rockets. It had come quietly until it simply was there. She loved Jake. And she felt his pain as if it were her own.

He moved abruptly to sit forward and grip the key in the ignition. Without a word to her, he turned the key again, and after one second of hesitation the van motor turned over. She didn't even question it happening. Jake needed it to work. It worked. She accepted that as easily as she did this love, and the fact that all agreements with Cutter were off. She didn't care if she owed the man for the rest of her life, there was no way she could make Jake remember any more of his time as a hostage.

The truth was the only thing she had room for right now. Emma was right. As soon as she could, Jake was going to know the truth. He looked at her, his face touched by shadows as the last of the fireworks died out. "Get out," he said, the order more a plea.

She just sat there. "No."

He didn't try again. He jammed the van into reverse, swung out of the parking spot and raised dust as he drove through the crowded parking lot to the highway. When they reached the blacktop, the van's tires squealed on the pavement as Jake pressed the accelerator and drove off into the night.

By the time they got to the hotel in Bliss, Whitney was afraid that Jake would let her out, then take off. He swung onto the driveway and brought the van to a skidding stop by the entrance. Without a word, he got out, slammed the door, and Whitney saw him take the steps in one long stride. A moment later he disappeared inside.

She knew he wanted to do this alone, to ride it out, but she wasn't about to let him be alone right now. She got out of the van, ran to the entrance and, as she stepped inside, she found emptiness and silence.

She went through the lobby, down the hallway to Jake's room and didn't bother knocking before she opened the door. When she stepped into the shadowy room, she didn't see Jake. Then she caught a movement by the bed and turned. He'd taken off his T-shirt and cap, and he was pushing things into his duffel bag. He didn't look up when she closed the door and crossed to him.

"Jake?"

His hands stilled, but he didn't glance at her.

"I know what's going on," she said.

He dropped the clothes and his grip on the bag, then slowly looked up. "Why are you here?" His voice was rough and low in the shadowy room.

How could she tell him she didn't have a choice? That she loved him with a love that she didn't even know existed until now. "My car—"

"No. Why are you here in this room now? Why are you standing there knowing what I am, what I can become?"

"I want to help you," she said simply.

"There isn't anything to help. Don't you understand that whatever I was I'm not anymore? I'm like some shell of a human being. There's no point in me being on this earth."

His words sent a jolt through her, and she had to fight nausea. "Don't say that," she uttered.

"It's true. I don't belong anywhere. I can't be with anyone. There's nothing left."

She fought against the memories of Bob Fillerman, but the frustration and pain she had felt with him was nothing compared to what she felt now. She didn't have words to even describe what the idea of this world without Jake Hill in it could do to her. "You . . . you can't just give up. You have to fight."

"No, I don't. I don't have the strength to do it anymore. It's over."

No! she wanted to rage at him. No! She bit her lip hard. "You might end your pain, but it only starts the pain for anyone left behind." Her own past was there, hanging like a shroud around her. And she hated Fillerman for what he'd done, not just to her, but to his family and friends who had willed him to come back to them from his kidnapping. "It tears people apart. It leaves them with their own nightmares."

He turned from her and crossed to the doors. He clutched the door frame with one hand as he stared out into the night. "What do you know about those things?"

"I knew a man who went through what you did, maybe more, maybe less. I don't know, but when he came back, he couldn't deal with it and he wouldn't ask for help."

"Everyone has to do things their own way," he whispered.

She bit her lip. "He did it his way, all right. He went to his hotel room and jumped out of the window. He got away from all the hurt, but the people he left behind didn't. I could hate him for that. And I've hated myself ever since, because I couldn't do anything to stop him."

The truth sat in front of her, words she didn't know were in her until they were said, spelling it out so clearly that she finally understood. She'd never been able to forgive herself for letting it happen.

"No one can stop a man if he doesn't want to be stopped," Jake murmured.

Another truth that she hadn't been able to accept until this moment. She couldn't stop Jake if he wouldn't let her. But she wouldn't give him up without a fight. "But they can try. Tell me what to do to help you."

"Let me go," he whispered, the words a heart-breaking plea. "Just let me go."

"I can't." She crossed to him. "I can't."

He didn't move. But he didn't run. "You have to. I can't pull you into my life."

She touched him and felt him start, but she didn't pull back. Gently she touched the irregularities of the scars on his back and whispered, "Are you going to let him win?"

"Let who win?"

"The man who did this to you?"

"Him? He won even when I killed him."

"No, he didn't. You're alive and he's dead." She leaned forward and touched her lips to his back. "You're alive," she breathed against his skin.

She felt him tremble, but he didn't turn to her. "Don't," he rasped.

But she didn't stop. She touched his scars, wishing she could take them away with her touch, and take away the horrors that had produced them. "Jake, let me stay with you."

Slowly he turned, and when his hands touched her shoulders she thought he was going to push her away. But he held on to her instead and his voice was a rough whisper. "I'll destroy you."

All she knew was it would destroy her if she had to leave him now. She touched her hands to his chest and felt his heart hammering under her palms. "I don't believe that."

His fingers tightened on her, hovering just this side of pain. "I'm not capable of anything else."

"Oh, yes, you are," she whispered and pressed her lips to his chest. She felt him tense, but she wasn't going to walk away and give up. There was nothing he could do to make her go, not now. She looked up at him. "I'm staying."

"No, you—" The words were cut off when she came even closer and pressed her hips against his.

"Yes," she murmured.

Jake didn't know what frightened him more. Whitney going, or Whitney staying. He stood very still as she came closer, her arms slipping around his waist, and her breasts against his chest. "I'm here. I'm staying," she whispered and touched her lips to the hollow at his throat.

Whatever strength it would have taken to physically put her out of his room was greater than he possessed. When her lips trailed over his skin, when she found his nipple and teased it into a hard nub with her tongue, he knew what he wanted.

He surrounded her with his arms, sealing her to him with that simple action, and there was no going back. For now, until it was gone, he wanted to know everything about Whitney, to explore every part of her and find the secrets that he knew were waiting for him. She melted against him, her slender body fitting so neatly against him he thought they could have been made for this moment.

With a groan, he gave in to the hunger for this woman that had burned in him for what seemed an eternity. His hand found her chin, cupping it to lift her face so he could find her mouth with his. And when their lips met, the caress was overwhelming, with her mouth opening to him, and his tongue trailed over her teeth, tasting and searching.

Her hand worked its way between them, and he drew in a sharp breath when he felt her fingers work-

ing under his waistband. The button on his jeans
snapped with a sharp sound, then the zipper gave and
her hand found him through the cotton of his under-
wear.

He closed his eyes tightly, and his lips stilled on hers.
He was incapable of doing anything but absorbing the
rocking shock of her touch on him. And the knowledge that her touch was what he'd been waiting for all
his life. No other woman existed for him. Whitney
blotted them all out. And as she slid her hand up and
down over the cotton, white fire exploded in him.

With a low groan he rocked toward her, then knew
that he needed skin against skin, touching Whitney
without any barriers and her touching him. He eased
back, the sight of her eyes heavy with desire only
stoking his own passion, and he quickly stepped out
of his boots and stripped off his jeans.

Without a word, Whitney tugged her top over her
head and let it drop to the floor, then she looked at
Jake and undid the button on her shorts. In one fluid
movement, she slid the white material down to her
ankles, then stepped out of it and nudged it away with
her foot. In that moment, as she stood before him in
a delicate white bra and bikini panties, Jake hesitated.

She was so delicate, so vulnerable, then she put her
hands behind her back and undid the snap on her bra.
Slowly the thin straps slipped off her shoulders and her
breasts fell free of the lacy fabric. Whitney never took
her eyes off Jake as she took off her panties and
stepped out of them. As she let the bra and panties fall
to the floor, she stood before Jake, with no embarrassment.

The sight of her was almost too much for him. With unsteady hands, he reached out and cupped her full breasts, his thumbs gently caressing her nipples to taut peaks. Her face flushed, and her sighs of pleasure ran wildly over his nerves.

He felt Whitney touch his waist, then work her fingers under the band of his shorts. She tugged them down until he was free of the binding material and there was nothing between the two of them anymore. His strength pressed against her abdomen, and she wrapped her arms around his neck, drawing him down to her.

"Take me to bed," she whispered against his mouth. "Your bed."

She didn't have to ask him twice. In one easy movement, he swept her high into his arms and crossed to the bed with her. With one foot, he kicked the duffel bag out of the way, and as she pressed her lips to the wildly beating pulse in his throat he slowly eased her down on the bed with him. He never let go of her, angling down by her until they were face-to-face in the coolness of the linen, and his clothes were brushed to the floor. Her breasts were against his chest, her hips aligned with his and their legs tangled together.

He kissed her long and deep, drugging himself with her essence, and his hand traced the swelling of her hips, his fingers exploring every curve. Then he found the line of her stomach, splaying his fingers on her abdomen, then moved lower to find the center of her being. As he cupped her, she arched toward him and pressed against his palm. Slowly he moved back and forth, hearing her sighs, then her head went back, her eyes closed, her cheeks flushed.

Her breathing was rapid, her own movements matching his until she covered his hand with hers to stop the motion. When he stilled, her hand shifted to him, circling him, her fingers slipping over his swelling, and when he knew he couldn't take it any longer he shifted over her.

Bracing himself with his hands flat on the pillow by her head, he touched her heat, tentatively, until she looked up at him over her. Her blue eyes were dark with desire, and her tongue touched her lips. "Please," she whispered. "I want you."

He tested himself against her, then slowly filled her, letting her velvet sheath close around him. And for a second he couldn't move. The idea of completion settled into his soul. A healing in some way. But before he could fully explore it, Whitney raised her hips and began to rock. With each movement, sensations rocked Jake, and he began to thrust, slowly at first, then faster and deeper.

His movements matched hers, and every part of him was centered in this room, with this woman under him. And with each motion that drew him against her, with every plunge into her, that was all that mattered. Here. Now. Whitney. As the intensity grew into an exquisite agony that promised a pain that had nothing to do with hurting, Jake felt Whitney wrap her legs around his hips, helping him fill her more completely.

When he heard her cry out for him, he went with her, letting the sensations drive him to an apex that pushed the world away and left the two of them to-

gether. He felt the contractions of her pleasure, and he
was propelled into a place of exquisite satisfaction
where only he and Whitney could go. And his only
thought was he loved Whitney. And heaven help him.

Chapter 12

Whitney woke from a deep, satisfying sleep with a feeling of loss. At first she didn't understand, but as she shifted in bed she knew. Jake was gone.

The thought jarred her into complete wakefulness, and she opened her eyes to the shadowy room. The heat of the evening lingered everywhere, and the sounds of night drifted in through the open doors. Whitney shifted as she looked around the room, then saw Jake in the shadows by the doors.

He sat on the tile floor, his back against the door frame, one leg stretched out, the other bent and his hand rested on his knee. Wearing only his briefs, he was staring at her, his hair falling forward to partially hide his face.

The limited light from outside barely defined his naked shoulders and chest, and his eyes were darkly unreadable. But she could feel the intensity of his gaze on her, and it made her mouth go dry. Her body still held the lingering traces of their lovemaking, and she craved his touch.

For several minutes she just lay there silently, looking at him and feeling his eyes on her, letting the wonder of loving him settle in. And as that solidified, she knew that the truth about everything came with that love. She couldn't let the lies and deception keep going. Finally she raised herself on one elbow, the light sheet falling back to expose her breasts. "Hello, there," she whispered.

"Hello."

"What are you doing over there?"

"Watching you and thinking."

"What are you thinking about?"

He tucked his hair back behind his ears and the softness of the night touched his face, shading hollows at his jaw and throat. "That I hardly know you."

"What do you want to know about me?"

"Nothing more." He looked away and out into the night. "It's better that way."

A chill skimmed over her despite the heat, and she found herself reaching for the sheet. She covered her breasts and clutched the cotton in her hand. All the fragile good feelings that had begun to grow were turning to powder. "Why?"

He flicked his hand dismissively. "It makes it easier."

"What easier?"

"Leaving."

The single word struck Whitney so hard she felt herself gasp for air. She sat up and stared at him, knowing she had dared to think he might want to stay, that he might want to find a way to make this work for longer than one night. "I'm not leaving," she said.

He turned back to her, and she hated not being able to see his eyes clearly. "I am."

"I thought—"

"Don't," he said abruptly.

She was unable to move for what seemed forever, then she found the strength to get out of bed. She tugged the sheet free and, with it in front of her, she crossed to where Jake sat. She stopped within two feet of him, then dropped to her haunches. "Don't what?" she asked, hating the unsteadiness in her voice.

"Don't do this."

She held to the sheet so tightly her hands were tingling. "What is it I'm doing?"

"Letting yourself pretend that this is all a fairy tale of some sort."

"It's a fairy tale to think you can pretend that none of this happened," she whispered.

"You're right," he murmured and rested his head back against the door frame, his eyes narrowed by his lowered lashes. "But that doesn't change anything."

She bit her lip so hard she was sure she'd make it bleed. "It doesn't change anything?" she finally echoed, knowing this night with Jake had changed everything for her.

"I'm a selfish bastard. I know that. This should never have happened."

Words that tore at her were said in a flat tone that ate at her nerves. "But it did."

He exhaled harshly. "I thought I'd made myself clear, that I'm not any good for anyone." He moved his hand sharply. "Hell, I can't even sleep with you around."

"Won't you try?"

"I can't take the chance."

She reached out and touched his hand resting on his knee, in some way hoping to reach him emotionally as well as physically. He flinched at the contact, but didn't move from it. "Jake, you have to let go of the past."

"Sure. Let go. Forget it. Just get on with living. I tried that. It didn't work."

She kept her hold on him, trying to will the barriers that she thought had begun to crumble during their lovemaking to stay down. But she could almost feel them rebuilding stone by horrible stone. "Maybe you need to forgive yourself."

"I told you, I never meant for all this to happen."

"That's not what I meant. You have to forgive yourself for living when that man died. I told you I carried around a whole lot of guilt about Bob Fillerman's death."

He laughed, a short, humorless sound. "There's a great difference between suicide and murder." He grimaced, then drew his hand back from hers, and she could feel another brick being put back in place. "Monumental."

She heard the muffled ringing of the phone in her room and it jarred her. Cutter. She hadn't contacted him for too long and he was edgy. Or maybe something else had happened with the ambassador. But she couldn't think of that now. Nothing mattered except Jake and her being here with him.

She sank down on the floor swaddled in the sheet and never took her eyes off Jake. "You never told me how those people took you in the first place."

He drew both knees to his chest and circled them with his arms. And for a very long time he just sat there. She was sure he was going to ignore what she'd said, but after taking an unsteady breath he finally said, "I was working on a deal for my company and the deal was done. I was on my way to the airport, but I didn't get past the street outside my hotel. There were others with the man, maybe three or four others, but I only saw him. He walked up to me on a busy street, pushed a gun in my face and forced me into a car."

"Didn't anyone try to help?" she asked, thankful when the phone stopped ringing.

"No. I don't know if anyone even noticed."

"Why did they pick you?"

"They're a fringe group of terrorists called the Light of Man, and I guess they thought they could use me to get money for the cause. They knew the company I worked for could produce millions if it had to. What they didn't know was the company also had a firm no-ransom policy."

"The company didn't help you at all?"

"Sure, they tried. They worked on it from their end, couldn't do anything, and they finally got in touch with the government." He shrugged, a sharp movement in the soft light. "It didn't matter. I knew I was on my own as soon as the terrorists blindfolded me and pushed me into the trunk of a car. Hours later when we finally stopped, they got me out, stripped me and threw me into a room of some sort. I called it 'the hole' because that's what it was. Dirt and wood and rocks and a smell that brought you to your knees." His hand clenched. "I wasn't the first one they had there."

"There were others?"

"I found gouges in the door, and places where someone had dug into the dirt wall and hit rock."

Cutter had been right. And the ambassador was probably in the same hole. "How long did they have you?"

"One hundred and ninety-one days and nights."

"Then you escaped?"

"I planned my escape a thousand times, but when it happened, it just happened. I couldn't take it anymore, and I struck out. I grabbed the guy when he came to...do his thing. I think I was going to beat him to death. But he wouldn't die, so I strangled him. I wasn't really proficient at it, so it took a while, but I finally killed him."

He lifted his hands, palms up, in front of him and stared at them. "There was blood everywhere, his and mine, and I broke a lot of bones in my hands. The human hand isn't meant to kill, actually." He slowly lowered his hands to his knees. "The ironic thing is the man I killed probably went to paradise for being a martyr for his cause, and I ended up in a living hell."

She leaned toward him, taking a chance of touching his hand again. "Jake, he was going to kill you."

"Sure. I keep telling myself that." He exhaled on a low hiss. "I told myself that very thing while I ripped the pants and shirt off his dead body and put them on. And when I pushed him into 'the hole' and threw the bolts on the door."

He fell silent, staring off into the shadows, his jaw working with tension.

"Jake, it was self-protection. You had to get out of there."

"Yeah," he murmured and slowly turned his hand over and laced his fingers with hers in a tight grip. "I had to get out of there."

He looked at her hand in his and spoke in a low, rough voice. "They'd kept me outside a little village in the hills, and I found out later it was pretty close to the Turkish border. For a day I walked, fell, got up, ran, fell, but kept walking. I finally met up with an old man on the road. He freaked out at first. He didn't speak English, and I must have terrified him. I was filthy, I smelled, my hair was matted and my beard was caked with dirt and blood from the fight."

"What happened with him?"

"I was lucky he was one of the locals who actually liked Americans. When he found out I was one, he gave me a ride and ended up smuggling me across the Turkish border hidden in a load of goats. He hooked me up with a cousin of a cousin of a cousin of someone. They took me to the outskirts of Ankara and dropped me. I don't remember how I got to the gates of the American embassy there, but the next thing I knew I was in a Turkish hospital with some guy who said he was with our government asking me questions."

"You made it," she breathed. "It's over. It's done. All that matters is you survived."

He closed his eyes for a minute, then looked at her. "Sure I survived."

"I'm glad you did," she said softly, the most monumental understatement she'd ever uttered, and she moved closer to him. She let go of the sheet so that it fell around her knees, and she reached out to touch his face. Her fingers were unsteady on the beginnings of a new beard at his jaw, then she leaned toward him and touched his cool lips with hers. "Very glad," she breathed.

Jake tasted Whitney on his lips, then looked at her in front of him, her beauty breathtaking contrast to the ugliness that seemed to live in him. She touched him in such a basic way that it went past passion, past need and want. Even though his body was tensing, and he wanted her again, he knew she touched a wound that had been hurting for so long in him that he'd given up having the pain ever stop. But for now, for this moment in time, she could push it back with her presence.

"The past is gone, and you have to—"

"Shh," he whispered as he touched her full bottom lip with his finger and slowly moved it back and forth. "No more talking. We don't have a lot of time before morning."

"Don't say that."

He brushed back her clinging strands of hair. "If I learned one thing in my life, I learned that now is all there is. This moment. Tonight."

"What about tomorrow?"

He closed his eyes, then met her gaze and spoke words that were painful to utter. "I can't give you a tomorrow."

"Jake, you—"

He stopped words that would only make what he had to do more impossible. "I'll stay until the morning comes."

He saw the brightness in her eyes, knowing she was fighting tears, and he had to fight his own, the first time he'd even been close to crying that he could remember. "Just until morning," he said, the need to reinforce it in himself every bit as strong as his need to let her know he had nothing else to offer her.

"All right. We'll talk then," she whispered.

He wanted to say there was nothing else to talk about, that no words could make things right. But he didn't want to hear those words himself. He didn't want to let himself think there could be something beyond the morning when he knew how impossible that would be. So he drew her to him and took her with a long, slow, aching kiss.

This love he'd discovered would either be his salvation for the rest of his life, or his damnation. Right now he didn't care which it was. As she swayed toward him, he drew her to her feet and went back to the bed with her.

All he wanted was to stop thinking and let himself get lost in her heat and the joy of her closeness. As they tumbled into the cool linen together, he took her slowly and surely, memorizing every angle, every curve, every soft sigh, every gasp, each and every pleasure she gave him.

When she welcomed him deep in herself, each thrust only made him more and more a part of her. And when she pleaded for completion, he wanted nothing more himself. All the ugliness of the outside world was held at bay, all the pain and hurt and fear. And for that moment in time, he felt the wonder of complete, absolute perfection.

An eternity later, Jake lay with Whitney in the shadows, her hand resting over his heart, her thigh curled over his leg. He knew he should get up, that he shouldn't take any chances of falling asleep. But when she sighed and snuggled even closer, and he felt her breasts pressed to his side, he didn't move. Just a moment longer, he thought as he closed his eyes. Just until the feeling of her lying with him burned its way into his soul so he'd have it with him always.

Fear came with a suddenness that made Jake bitterly sick. He was in "the hole," lying facedown on the foul, damp-smelling ground, grit in his mouth and nose. A boot on his neck kept him pinned as a gun at his head clicked over and over again on empty chambers.

"You will die," the man hissed and the laughter rang out, a crazy, horrendous sound that held pure evil.

Rage consumed Jake, a rage that wouldn't flinch at killing, and he knew in the next instant he'd grab his tormentor by the throat and squeeze the life out of him.

Jake broke out of the nightmare and into consciousness so abruptly it stunned him. His body was rigid and soaked with moisture, and his breathing was ragged and rapid. Damn it, he'd let himself fall asleep. He'd let go and let the darkness creep into the bed with him and Whitney.

He didn't move. Whitney was nestled against his side with a familiarity that should have only come after years of loving someone. The room was touched by the pale grayness of dawn, and he knew morning was here, dragging reality along with it.

No matter what he'd let himself think fleetingly last night, he knew he had to get out of here. The dream proved that to him. This time he'd broken free of the nightmare before anything happened, but it could have been very different. He could have touched Whitney and hurt her, and he knew the motorcycle part would be in today when the delivery came. By the time the sun came up tomorrow, he knew he had to be miles from here and an eternity from Whitney.

It took all of his willpower to make himself slowly ease away from Whitney, and as he broke the contact she rolled away from him. With a sigh, she curled into a ball on her side.

Silently Jake stood, his sense of isolation a living thing now that he wasn't touching Whitney. He reached for his discarded jeans, pulled them on, put on a T-shirt, then pushed his feet into his boots. He reached for his duffel bag that had fallen on the floor and quickly stuffed his things in it helter-skelter. When Whitney stirred, Jake froze. He didn't move again until she settled, then he folded up his bedroll and tied it. He found his cap, tugged it on, slipped his duffel bag strap over one shoulder and grabbed his bedroll.

For one moment he let himself look at Whitney lying in his bed. This time it wasn't a trick of his eyes because of the weak morning light or an illusion of the shadows. She was as real as his love for her and as real as the knowledge he would hurt her if he stayed.

He turned, crossed to the patio doors and walked out. He'd go to the garage and wait until the delivery came with the motorcycle part. Going around to the front of the hotel, he passed his dead motorcycle and went to the van. He tossed his things in the side door before he went around and got in behind the wheel. He'd left the key in the ignition the night before, but when he turned it over nothing happened.

"Damn temperamental bucket of bolts," he muttered as he tried it over and over again. But it wouldn't start.

He sat back, stared out the window, then turned and climbed into the back of the van. He got his things, slid the side door open and got out. Taking his things back to the room was out of the question, so he crossed to where his bike was parked and put his bedroll and duffel bag behind a rock near the hitching post.

He turned and headed down the driveway on foot. Nothing was easy for him lately, he thought as he turned onto the main street and set off in the direction of the garage. The streets were empty, the sun barely touching the shadows of night that still lingered everywhere. The only sounds were the rustling of paper chased by a light morning breeze and the hum of insects in the warm air.

Emptiness was all around. Not a person was stirring and Jake felt that sense of isolation again. It had started when he looked down at Whitney as he left her in the bed, and now it grew. Before meeting her, he probably wouldn't have cared. Now it grew into an aching loneliness. A loneliness he was facing for the rest of his life.

"You have to forgive yourself." He could hear the echo of Whitney's words in his mind. *"Forgive yourself for living."*

As he neared the garage, he kicked at a tin can and it skittered along the wooden sidewalk and struck a signpost by the side of road. Forgiveness. He'd never thought about it in those terms. He'd never thought about any of this until Whitney had forced him to with her stubborn insistence on talking and hashing things over and over again. A trait that annoyed him, angered him, and a trait that touched him.

His steps slowed. Even if she was right, he didn't have any idea how to do it. One more thing she'd said that was making a lot of sense. He needed help. That was a monumental admission for him. But so was admitting that he loved Whitney.

He stepped into the parking area of the garage and headed past the gas pumps. As he neared the garage doors, he stopped and lifted his face to the rising sun. He felt the growing heat against his skin, and he inhaled the freshness in the air. God, he wished he was out for a walk in the early morning, taking a breather, then heading back to Whitney. He wished he wasn't running again, taking off until he found another town, another job, another place to wait until everything crumbled.

He was startled by a sound behind him, but before he could turn, something was pressed into his ribs and a voice hissed in his ear. "Get your hands where I can see them, and don't do nothing stupid."

As Jake eased his hands up, he saw the door to Wally's office was slightly ajar and the wooden frame was splintered by the lock. "Good," the man behind him said, then jabbed him sharply with the gun again. "Inside."

As Jake moved toward the door, he caught the reflection of the man behind him in the window glass. Maybe in his thirties, he wore a bandanna tied into a skullcap over dark hair, had a scraggly beard and his eyes were wide and intense. Then the man shoved Jake in the back and sent him forward into the door. The barrier gave way, and Jake stumbled over the doorjamb, half falling into the darkened office.

As he righted himself by grabbing the desk edge, he looked up and saw someone else in there, another man in the shadows. Suddenly a bright light blinded Jake, and the man behind him struck him in the shoulder, sending pain radiating through his body. The past was suddenly there, taking over, smothering out the present with fear and burning rage that threatened to consume Jake.

He was back in "the hole" being beaten, blinded by light, the fury building in him, his hatred for his tormentor a living thing. His right wrist was grabbed and his hand twisted behind his back, threatening to dislocate his shoulder. The pain took over, and Jake heard deafening voices, different, yet all from the same man.

"What in the hell?"

"Look what I found outside."

"Get rid of him."

"No problem." The gun was at the base of his neck, the barrel cold and hard.

He was going to die. With an animalistic scream, Jake jerked his hand free, paying the price of pain searing down his arm and into his shoulder. He rammed his elbow back into his captor's stomach and, as the gun went off, Jake lunged across the desk to grab the other man by his shirt.

In one motion, Jake jerked the man to one side and smashed him face first into the desk. Blood sprayed everywhere, but Jake didn't notice its stain on his hands or on the whiteness of his T-shirt. All he knew was the one with the gun was making a break for it.

Jake ran for the door. When he charged outside, he was back in the village, at the bottom of the muddied ramp that went down to "the hole." He rushed after the man, grabbing him before he could get far from the entrance to "the hole." They fell forward, and Jake got on top. He hated the voice, the pain, and he hated the man for everything he'd taken from him.

Whitney woke to the discomfort of a too-warm room, the sheet sticking to her bare skin and a sense of foreboding that made no sense. Until she reached for Jake and found nothing but mussed sheets and an empty space where he'd lain during the night. She pushed herself up, pushed the sheets off and glanced around the room awash in the light of dawn.

Her foreboding only grew when she realized Jake's clothes, which had been scattered on the floor last night, were gone. She couldn't see his duffel bag or bedroll, and as she scrambled out of bed to check in the bathroom she breathed, "No, please, no." She hurried over to the open patio doors and touched the door frame as she looked out at the early morning, washed in pale pink and mauve. The patio and terrace were silent and empty.

Standing very still, she couldn't sense Jake at all, and someway she knew if he was close by she'd feel it. *"Until the morning comes."* Jake had said it, and he'd meant it. She was the one who'd fooled herself. Jake never had. Morning had come, and he was gone. He'd left.

She closed her eyes and slowly sank to the tile floor, her back against the door frame in the same place Jake had sat last night while he fought sleep. She knew that part of her had thought that making love would bind him to her, that loving him would hold him close.

"Stupid," she muttered as she drew her knees up and pressed her forehead to them. She'd been stupid to let Cutter send her here. She'd been stupid to lie to Jake. It hadn't done anyone any good. She hadn't found out anything substantial to help the ambassador. Jake was out there alone again and still in pain. And now she was alone.

She was startled by the sound of sirens cutting through the stillness, so close that the shrill noise seemed to make the air vibrate. As the first siren started to fade out, another one took its place, then another one and Whitney could hear someone yelling. The words were indiscernible, but she could hear the urgency in them.

She got to her feet, dressed quickly, then hurried out into the hall. As she ran toward the lobby, Maria appeared and called to her, "Something has happened in town. There are police everywhere."

Then the door opened and someone called, "It's Wally's garage. The cop's are all over it."

Whitney broke into a run, passing Maria to get to the door and get out onto the porch. Some people were hurrying past on the street as the last of the sirens died out. "Where are Wally and Emma?" she asked.

Maria was behind her. "I do not know."

Whitney started down the steps toward the van. "I'll go and see what's going on."

She saw Jake's bike still parked by the hitching post. He'd left without it, so taking the part hadn't really helped at all. She got in the van, started it and headed for the garage.

When she got close, she saw three police cars parked in the parking lot, their lights flashing, and people were gathering near the street. Whitney stopped the van in front of the restaurant, got out and ran toward the garage. As she pushed her way through the onlookers, she broke out into the parking area of the garage.

She stopped dead, stunned to see two policemen with their guns drawn and pointed at Jake, who was on the ground straddling a man who was frantically trying to pull Jake's hands off his throat. A sheriff had Jake by the shoulders, yelling at him, "Enough! Get off of him, man, and do it now!"

Whitney took one look at Jake, and she knew that whatever had happened here Jake was lost in the past. He was fighting the terror and pain as if it all centered in the man under him.

Chapter 13

Whitney saw the cop let go of Jake's shoulders, then move to the right. The next thing she knew, he had a black club in his hands and he swung it sideways, striking Jake in his jaw. For a split second, everything seemed to stop, then Jake swayed and fell sideways onto the gravel. The man under him twisted away, freeing himself and gasping for air as he held his throat.

Whitney tried to get to Jake, but when she got within five feet of him someone put out an arm and stopped her. "Stay back, miss."

She stopped, vaguely aware of people rushing around, more sirens, someone yelling about another man in the office and police radios crackling. But all she saw was Jake awkwardly push himself up with one hand, then sink back against the concrete of the gas pump island for support. One hand touched his jaw, testing it, smearing the trickle of blood at the corner of his mouth. He drew back his hand and stared at it, then looked up at the crowd that was gathering.

Whitney pushed at the arm restraining her and got past, but before she could get to Jake a cop grabbed him by his arm. He jerked him to his feet, but the other man was still on the ground with two men in white bending over him. The cop took out a pair of handcuffs and pulled Jake's left hand out, and as the it closed with a click Jake muttered, "You got this all wrong."

"Looked to me like you were trying to kill this guy," the sheriff said. "You aren't going to tell me you were just out here giving him a wrestling lesson, are you?"

Jake stared at the man he'd attacked as two men helped him to his feet. "He and the guy inside were robbing the place."

"That ain't so," the man on the ground said. "It was him." He was still holding his throat, but glaring at Jake. "I was just passing by, and I saw what he was up to. I was trying to stop him when he went frigging crazy and tried to kill me."

Any innocent person would have been screaming denial by then, but Jake just stood there staring at the man, not uttering a word.

"There's been a break-in," someone called from the office area. "There's another guy in here all bloodied up, and the place is a mess."

"Looks as if we've got a problem here." The sheriff looked at Jake, then at the other man. "I think we'll all take a ride to the station. A bit of time locked up can make things remarkably clear."

Whitney saw Jake blanch and she cut in. "No. You can't do that."

The sheriff turned and looked at her. "What are you talking about?"

There was no way Jake could survive being locked in a cell. Just being in the van had driven him to roll down the windows. Being in his hotel room had made him open all the doors. He'd die from it. "You can't do that. He's not involved in anything."

"Did you see what happened here?"

"No, but—"

His eyes narrowed on her. "You were in on this?"

"No, of course not. But—"

"Then what in the hell do you know about it?"

"I know him." She glanced at Jake, his dark eyes unblinking, watching her. "He works here," she said. "Just go and find the owner, Wally Lanier. He's probably out where they had the rodeo and carnival yesterday. Send someone out to get him. He'll tell you."

"Just because this guy's working for Wally doesn't mean he isn't trying to rip him off."

"But he's not. I give you my word, he's not."

"You got some ID?"

"No, it's at the hotel. But if you get Wally, I'm sure he—"

The cop shook his head. "We'll sort this out at the station."

She could feel Jake's tension growing with each word the man uttered. Then she knew what she had to do. There was nothing between herself and Jake to salvage, so there was no reason to lie any longer. It wouldn't protect anyone, and only hurt him. "Wait, please."

The sheriff exhaled with obvious exasperation. "Lady, I can't—"

"If you'll just make one call for me, we can get this all settled . . . without you making a terrible mistake."

"What mistake would that be?"

"Locking up a man who stopped a robbery rather than committed one."

The man hesitated. "What call?"

"Call Cutter Ford in Washington, D.C." She spoke quickly, trying not to look at Jake as she gave the policeman Cutter's number. "Tell him that Whitney Tate needs verification that Jake Hill is under his protection and isn't to be detained."

The sheriff frowned. "You're saying this guy's with the government?"

"No. Just call Cutter Ford. Please."

While he told one of the policemen by the nearest police car to make the call, Whitney chanced a look at Jake. She was braced for anger, for accusations, for being hit hard by her own betrayal.

But he wasn't even looking at her. He stared at the ground. He didn't look up. He didn't speak. He didn't move. And she couldn't do a thing but wait. Finally the call came over the radio and the cop by the squad car called out to the one by them. "Ford vouched for both of them. The lady works for him, and she's working with Mr. Hill. He's not to be detained. Ford says he'll take full responsibility for both of them."

"I'll be damned," the sheriff muttered as he undid his handcuffs. "Looks as if you're out of here, buddy. We'll be in touch for a statement from you later on."

Jake rubbed at his wrists, then walked away without a look at Whitney.

She went after him, and as they neared the van she called out, "Jake, I've got the van. I'll drive you back." But he didn't stop. He just kept walking away from her.

Whitney grabbed the key out of the van, then ran after him. The sun was up now and heat was beginning to build. After a painfully silent walk back to the hotel, she was hot and breathless. But as she followed Jake up the driveway, she couldn't stand the silence any longer. "Jake?"

He acted as if she hadn't spoken and took the porch steps in one stride. As he reached for the door, she ran after him and said, "Jake. We have to talk."

At the door, he stopped, and she could see him take a deep breath before he turned. His face looked oddly pale, and his eyes were narrowed as if he couldn't quite look at her directly. "Go ahead, talk. Tell me about you and Cutter Ford, and why he sent you out here. He did send you, didn't he?"

"Yes, but—"

"You work for him?"

"No. I mean, I did, but I don't usually."

She could see his hands clench at his sides. "Don't play word games with me. Just tell me what's going on."

She exhaled and brushed at her face, at the moisture that dampened her skin in the heat. "Can we go inside?"

"*We* aren't going anywhere. Just tell me the truth."

She flinched at the cold edge to his tone. "All right. I used to work for Cutter, and when I needed to change jobs he helped me get another one. One day he walked into my office and said he needed me to do something for him, that I owed him."

"What was it?"

"He needed help."

"With what?"

"Getting you to talk."

He stared at her. "What?"

"He'd sent people to find you before, and you walked out on them."

"There was nothing to talk about. I told them that. I didn't want any part of the government's feeble attempts to make sense out of what happened to me. It didn't make sense. It won't make sense even if you put the whole CIA on it. Especially not if they sent a blonde to get close to me."

His sarcasm cut. "Cutter would have sent anyone he could get to come here. I'm only here because I owed him and I could get clearance fast."

"What in the hell do I have that he wants badly enough to send troops after me?" he demanded roughly.

"An American ambassador's been taken hostage by the same people who took you. There's no trace of where they're keeping him, and Cutter thinks you might know something that could help."

"Oh, God. They took another one," he whispered.

"Yes, they did. Cutter sent me to find out what I could."

He slowly shook his head. "And you're good at what you do, aren't you?"

"I'm not. That's why I quit as a debriefer. Right now I'm in over my head, and I hate lies, but I was trying to help."

"By giving your all for your country?"

She flinched at that. "No, it wasn't like that."

"Bull," he muttered and jammed his hands into the pockets of his jeans.

The door opened and Maria looked outside. "Oh, you are back. I heard on the telephone about the robbery." She shook her head. "It is a terrible thing."

"Yes, it is," Whitney murmured, knowing how terrible things happened in this world. She realized she was still holding the key to the van. "Here," she said, holding it out to the woman. "The keys to the van. Give them to Wally or Emma when they get back."

Maria stepped out and took the keys, then fumbled in the pocket of her apron and held something out to Whitney. "I found this in your room when I was cleaning, and I did not know if it was important. I thought I should give it to you."

Whitney looked at the part from Jake's bike in the woman's hand, and she felt sick. "Thank you," she managed, not caring that her hand was shaking as she took it from her. And beyond hoping to hide the sight from Jake.

"Will either one of you be wanting breakfast?" the woman asked.

"No, thanks," Whitney said.

"No," Jake murmured.

As the door closed behind Maria, Whitney made herself look back at Jake. He held out his hand without a word, and she dropped the part in his palm. She accidentally brushed his hand with her finger and he jerked back as if she'd burned him.

"Damn you," he hissed and turned to reach for the door. But before he left, he turned to cast her a cutting look. "If Ford wants to ask me questions, you tell him to come here and face me, and not to send someone like you to do his dirty work." Then he went in the hotel and slammed the door after him.

Whitney crossed to the swing and sank down on it, her legs weak and unsteady from the confrontation. It was over. Just like that. Done. She ran an unsteady hand over her face and stared out at the heat beginning to shimmer in the air. And she didn't have anything to show for it but her own sense of failure and the knowledge that she'd found something here that she'd never had before. And she'd lost it.

As the heat grew, she got up and went into the dim coolness of the hotel. Walking through the empty lobby, she headed down the hall to her room. She'd pack and try to find a car to rent, then get out of here.

She went into her room, a room not touched with memories of last night, and closed the door. The hum of the air conditioner was the only sound as Whitney crossed to the bed and began to strip off her clothes. But as she turned to go into the bathroom in her bra and panties, the phone rang. She stared at it for three rings, tempted to just ignore it the way she had during the night, but she knew she couldn't.

She reached for it, gripping the cold plastic, and she pressed it to her ear. "Yes?"

"That man is on the telephone for you again," Maria said.

"Put him through."

There was a double click, then an open line. "Cutter?"

"All right, what was that all about?"

She sank down on the side of the bed and told him about the robbery and about Jake. But as she spoke the words, she knew she was telling him a story about a man on the edge. She didn't give a hint how close she was to that edge herself.

"He knows everything?" Cutter asked.

"Yes."

"And?"

"He said if you want to know anything, you have to come here, face him yourself and ask."

"I'll be there as soon as I can."

"I can't guarantee he'll be here when you arrive."

"Just stay put and wait for me. I'll find you at the hotel as soon as I can."

Before she could say anything else, the line clicked and Cutter was gone. Slowly she put the phone back in the cradle, then she got up and went into the bathroom. She turned on the shower, then stepped under the spray. She normally wasn't a weepy person. But the first time she'd cried in a very long time was here in this shower. And the tears came again now, mingling with the water.

But this time they were tears of grief, tears of loss, and she let them fall until she couldn't cry anymore. When she got out and wrapped a towel around her, she went into the bedroom and lay down on the bed. She'd barely settled when she heard the door to Jake's room open and close.

A few minutes later she heard the motorcycle start, and she closed her eyes tightly. The sound revved, then faded off into the distance. Knowing Jake had driven away seemed anticlimactic to the moment she'd found him gone early this morning. And the rest of the day seemed like a dream, a nightmare, some odd footnote to the pain she'd experienced at dawn.

She rolled onto her side and closed her eyes. She'd told Cutter she couldn't guarantee Jake being here when he got here. And she wasn't going to go after Jake again. Either he would be here for Cutter or he wouldn't be. There wasn't anything she could do about that, not any more than she could stop loving him.

Whitney stayed in her room until someone knocked on her door in the early afternoon. When she opened the door, she found Emma there in a flowing white caftan, her face flushed. "Maria said you haven't been out since you got back from the garage, and I got worried about you."

"I'm all right. Just tired, I guess."

"I don't doubt it after what all happened here. Goodness, we get a police car coming after us with its sirens going and find out that the garage has been broken into. And for them to accuse Jake of doing it, it's just crazy. But the county sheriff just doesn't know people like a local would. He just figured he'd take them all in and see what happened."

"He didn't know what was going on."

She studied Whitney. "He said you got someone from Washington, D.C., to vouch for Jake. That Mr. Ford?"

"Yes. I didn't have a choice."

"And that's why he's leaving, isn't it?"

"Yes. But he's left already."

"Oh, no, honey, he's down at the station with Wally still. Wally's trying to get him to stay."

He hadn't left, after all, at least not yet, and she had hope that he was waiting around for Cutter to show up. "Jake's really at the garage?"

"Yeah, for now. But he's definitely going. I hate to see him do it, on a purely selfish level. If it wasn't for him those two jerks that tried to rob us would have gotten away with it."

"Who were they?"

"Drifters who wandered into town, probably on drugs. They must have figured after the celebration yesterday no one would be up and around so early." She frowned. "They didn't figure on Jake's insomnia."

"Did Jake say exactly when he was leaving?"

"No, just that since he got his bike working, he's ready to head out." She studied Whitney. "You look as if you need a bite to eat. I'll send Maria in with something for you."

Emma would have turned and left if Whitney hadn't spoken to her. "Emma, I'm going to have a visitor later."

"That Mr. Ford?"

"Yes, he's coming out himself to see if he can do any good."

"When he gets here, I'll make sure you know."

"Thanks."

"One more thing—"

"What is it?"

"I don't have any gift like Wally does, or like Grace does, and I'm sure no fortune teller, but if I was you, I'd be right there when Mr. Ford finds Jake. And I'm not at all sure I'd be walking off with Mr. Ford when it was all over.''

"I don't have a choice about being here," she said.

"Maybe not, but you've got a choice about letting everything slip through your fingers."

Whitney met the woman's gaze and she knew that Cutter Ford had no corner on looking into souls. "He doesn't want me," she whispered.

"He doesn't know what he wants. That's pretty obvious."

"But he's—"

"He's still here. He didn't run away immediately. Maybe he doesn't need a broken van or magic to stay for just a bit longer. And maybe this isn't the time for you to walk away and live with regrets for the rest of your life."

It had been hard doing that since Bob Fillerman's death, and Whitney knew that a lifetime of regret wasn't living. "Thanks, Emma."

"You just think about it, and when your boss gets here you be ready to do what you want."

Whitney watched Emma go off down the hall, then she went back into her room and shut the door. A lifetime of regret, and a lifetime of memories for company. Whitney trembled, then hugged her arms around herself. She'd be ready when Cutter got here.

Somewhere deep in the hotel a clock chimed the hour of seven while Whitney sat on the front porch of the hotel on the old swing. Despite her decision to not let go easily, Whitney finally accepted the fact that Jake was gone. He'd never come back from the garage, and when Wally came to pick up Emma to go and say their goodbyes to Grace and Les, he'd told Whitney Jake had driven off.

After Emma and Wally left, Whitney had come out here to wait for Cutter and give him the news that had left her numb. With her knees pulled to her middle and her arms around them, she watched the road and finally she saw lights coming down the street.

She sat a bit straighter as the lights slowed, then swung toward the hotel and came up to the entrance. When the dark sedan stopped, Whitney watched Cutter step out and turn to look over the car hood at the hotel. "Whitney?"

She sat up, putting her feet on the floor and said, "What took you so long?"

"Bad weather and bad luck." He closed the door and came around to the porch steps. Dressed in a rumpled shirt and slacks, he looked harried and pressured. And that made her uneasy. "Got the charter, then got grounded for weather twice." He stopped and looked down at her. "Where's Hill?"

She shrugged. "I don't know. He told the man at the garage that he was leaving today, and I haven't seen him since before I talked to you."

"Where's the garage? Maybe the owner knows where Hill was heading."

"He doesn't. He said his goodbyes and left. They don't know where he went."

"That's another thing I don't understand. How in the hell did he get his bike going?"

"He found a used part," she said, not about to explain what happened. "What now?"

"We start looking. He might be close by. Did he get to know anyone while he was here?"

"No." She swung back and forth on the swing. "He's pretty isolated."

"Anything he spoke about wanting to do?"

She stood and walked to the edge of the porch. "No, nothing."

"Did he tell you any more about his captivity?" Cutter asked from behind her.

"He was kept near to the Turkish border, in the low mountains, in a mud and wood hole in the ground. I think it was outside a village, or at least pretty isolated from the people nearby. He went a long ways after escaping before he met up with a local who didn't hate Americans. That man took Jake across the border in a load of goats. From there he made connections to Ankara. That's about it."

"Any names, or any actual locations?"

"No, not really," she said, then hesitated as she saw something near a rock by the hitching post where Jake had kept his motorcycle. She stepped off the porch and went to look. When she got close, she felt light-headed with relief. Jake wasn't gone. His bedroll and backpack were by a large rock. "He's still here," she told Cutter.

She heard Cutter coming up behind her. "What?"

She motioned to Jake's things on the ground. "That's all he's got. He wouldn't have left them. He must have stayed to talk to you. He said he would, if you came to him."

"Great. All we have to figure out is where he is."

Whitney knew. She turned to Cutter and said, "I'll take you to Jake."

Chapter 14

Jake heard the car motor just as the last rays of the sun fled, but he didn't move. He stayed on the edge of the drop-off by the burial grounds and stared at the valley far below. He'd wanted to get on his bike and go and never look back. But Whitney had robbed him of that option. And he knew she'd find him out here.

He heard footsteps on the rough ground behind him, then a man slipped into place beside him on the edge. "We don't need introductions, do we, Jake?" Cutter Ford asked.

"No, we don't."

"I'm sorry for doing this the way we did."

"Forget it." He didn't want to ask, but had to know. "Whitney told you where I'd be?"

"She figured it out."

"She's good at what she does for you," he murmured. "Very good."

"No, she's not. That's why she doesn't actually work for me anymore. She took the suicide of one of our sub...of a hostage we were debriefing, personally. She thought she should have been able to foresee it and stop it."

The man she'd told Jake about. And he'd thought the man might have been a lover.

"That made her ineffective. She got involved to the point that she felt responsible for the man. She didn't understand that you can't allow that to happen. You just do your job the best way you can. You lose a few, but you save some, too."

Jake cast the man a slanting glance, a bit surprised to see him out of the expected suit and tie. "You're a cold-blooded bastard, aren't you, Ford?"

The man didn't take offense. "It keeps me sane. Right now we're in a time crunch."

"The ambassador's either wishing he was dead, or he is dead and you're talking buzzwords."

"Bottom line, we need to get our people to him." Nothing affected this man. "You're the only one who's been where he's being kept. The only one who lived to tell about it, anyway. I need to find the man, Jake. I need to get him out."

"I told Whitney about all I remember," Jake said, turning back to the view spread out below. "It's more impressions and hallucinations than facts."

"Anything might help," Ford said. "Just tell me what you can."

Slowly Jake began to tell Ford what he remembered, and things he hadn't even been aware of knowing until they came to him. With Whitney, the thoughts had come at random, triggered by her presence and words, but with this man they were cold and factual. And for the first time since he'd made his escape, he felt as if he could remember without bringing on the nightmares and visions.

A truth came to him as he kept speaking. If it hadn't been for Whitney being here, he never would have been able to face this now. Because of the way Whitney prodded him and encouraged him, because of her gentleness and stubbornness, and her understanding, he could remember.

But that's what she was getting paid for by the man sitting next to him. That's why they were both here. Not out of some humanitarian gesture, or because of any other reason. They did a job. They got paid. "There isn't any more I can tell you," Jake finally said.

Ford stood and brushed at his slacks. "I thank you for doing this."

Jake glanced up at the man, the shadows of the coming night blurring his features. "Will this make the papers when it's settled?"

"I'll make sure it gets some coverage, no matter what. You'll find out what happens. Can I do anything for you?"

"No."

"If you want help, all you have to do is ask." He took a card out of his pocket and held it out to Jake. "My number. Wherever you go, just call. I'll do what I can. I know people who can work miracles with PTSD."

Jake took the card and pushed it into his pocket. "I'll watch the papers."

"Do you know where you're going from here?"

Jake had no place to go; he'd decided that just before Ford got here. He never really had, but he hadn't accepted that until right now. His running was over, because he only took his emotional baggage with him no matter where he went. "No, I don't."

"Well, take care of yourself. I'll be waiting for your call."

"Sure," Jake said and turned to the view.

He heard Cutter walk away, then get in the car, start the engine and drive off. Jake listened until its engine sounds died out, then all he had around him was space and emptiness.

He'd never felt so alone. And he knew that because of Whitney he'd never know what it was like not to be alone again. Strange that a heart could hurt, and he hadn't even thought he had a heart left until she appeared on the side of the road with her dead car.

The car. His hands clenched on his thighs. That had to be a plant, something arranged by Cutter Ford to give her a reason to contact him. Dammit, he couldn't just let it go. He couldn't just walk away. Something seemed to be pushing him to go back, to see her one more time and try to figure out where truth and lies had begun and ended.

This place was getting to him. He got to his feet and turned to go, but stopped when he saw someone coming toward him from the area of the burial grounds. In the dusky evening, he thought he was seeing things, that visions were coming to him in a different form now.

He saw something he wanted to believe in, but something he was terrified of believing in, in case it was all a product of his imagination.

But as Whitney came closer to him, and he saw her pale hair, her tiny figure in white shorts and a dark top, his whole body reacted in the most primitive way to the image. And he knew she was no mirage. She was real.

"Did you come up with Ford?" he asked.

"I showed him how to get here." Her voice came to him on the warm evening air, running havoc over his frayed nerves.

"He left."

"Yes, he has to get back and try to work things out."

"Why are you still here? I told him everything I can remember. There isn't any more."

"I told Cutter to go. I needed to stay for a while."

"Why?"

"I couldn't let things end the way they had. I had to explain, to try and make you see that I started this for Cutter. But I'm ending it for me."

"Ending it? Is that what this is all about, trying to end this so you can live with yourself, so you don't have to live with guilt the way you did with Fillerman's death?"

She stopped just a few feet from him, and he could see the tension touching her mouth and eyes. "I finally figured out how to live with my past mistakes, but I just can't figure out how to..."

She turned from him as her voice trailed off, and she went past him to the edge of the drop-off.

For a long moment she just stood there, her beauty touched by the gentleness of the coming night. And his hands ached to touch her.

"It's beautiful up here," she whispered. "Sort of magical."

He stayed where he was, never taking his eyes off her. "You can't figure out how to do what?"

She lifted her face to look up at the twilight sky. "The sky looks as if someone painted it with pastels, doesn't it?"

He persisted. "Do what?"

She hesitated, then turned and crossed to where he stood, keeping just inches of space between them. With a shake of her head, she said, "I need to tell you something."

He knew he should get out of here while he could still do it, but his legs felt as if they wouldn't carry him over the dusty ground to the motorcycle. "What's going on?" he asked, his voice hoarse.

"Jake, I started this for all the wrong reasons. I admit that. I really believed that Cutter blackmailed me into coming, but I finally figured out that I came because I thought I could help, and maybe make up for what happened to Bob Fillerman. It was guilt, then."

"What about now?"

She came closer, so near to him that he was bombarded with the delicate scent that clung to her. He could feel her heat along the length of his body, and it seemed that his body didn't really give a damn what she was or what she did. "Now? I'm afraid it's love."

He flinched at her words. "What?"

She touched him, resting her hands on his chest, and his feelings ran out of control. "I love you," she said softly, and he could have sworn she was bracing herself for a blow. "I'm not lying, I swear I'm not. And

I'm not here for Cutter. I'm here because I can't figure out how to make you believe that I love you."

He moved away from her, the words ringing in his mind, words that made his heart soar at the same time they scared him more than anything had before in his life. He found himself at the edge of the drop-off, the warm breeze skimming over his skin.

"Jake?" Whitney was right behind him, and his need to turn and hold on to her was almost a living thing.

"No, I . . . I—"

"Jake, if you don't love me, I'll let you go. Just tell me you don't love me."

He closed his eyes so tightly that colors exploded behind his lids. "Love you?" he whispered hoarsely.

"I promise I'll walk away, and you won't ever have to deal with me again. But I have to hear you say you don't love me." She laughed, an unsteady sound. "I'm too stubborn. I can't give up, not unless I know you don't care at all."

The thoughts he'd had before the robbery had seemed to taunt him. Could this ever stop with him? What if he couldn't be helped? What if he ever hurt her? "What if I do care?" He couldn't look at her. "What, then?"

The silence behind him ravaged his nerves, and just when he was about to tell her to forget it, to let him go, she said, "I'd love you more than I ever loved anyone in my life."

His throat ached. "But what if I can't forget? What if you're in love with a man who's claustrophobic?" His voice was shaking. "A man who can't sleep at night, a man who could hurt you?"

He felt her touch his back and the contact became the center of the universe. "Do you love me?"

"I do." He opened his eyes to the night where stars were just beginning to come to life. "I love you."

Her touch on him trembled, then she let him go. Without her touch, he felt lost. He was in darkness without a light. Turning, he saw her standing there, her eyes bright with tears that spilled down her cheeks and her hand pressed to her mouth.

"Oh, God, I don't want to hurt you," he whispered.

With a sob, she threw herself into his arms, holding to him so tightly that he could feel her trembling. "I love you. I love you," she sobbed.

He held to her, pressing his cheek to her hair and closing his eyes. "I just don't know if loving is enough."

She rubbed her forehead on his chest. "That's all there is," she said, her voice muffled. "All I can do is love you." She moved back enough to look up into his face, and her hand gently stroked his jawline. "I'll help you do whatever it takes to be well. I'll be there for you. If we have to camp out forever, we will. If you need to keep moving, we will. I'll do anything. And I'll love you. That's all I can promise."

Suddenly Jake knew that was all he needed. With Whitney he wasn't alone. He wasn't fighting demons in the dark. She was light, his light, and he whispered, "That's enough."

The kiss was long and searching, a seal to their commitment, and as Jake drew back, his hands framing Whitney's face, he asked, "Do you want to stay here until morning?"

She smiled, her cheeks damp, but her eyes alive with love. "I'm going to stay with you until forever."

December 24

Jake put the phone back in place and lay back in the bed, reaching out to pull Whitney to him. The soft glow from the side lamp touched her features, and if a man could have died from happiness he knew he was a goner.

"Who was that?" she asked, her voice making a vibration against his side.

"Cutter. He wanted to thank you for the gold-plated key you gave him for his town house." He smiled. "Did you really do that?"

"Sure." She touched her lips to his chest. "He needs to get a life before he's too old to enjoy it." She drew back and raised herself on one elbow to look at him. "What are you thinking about?"

He met her blue gaze and said honestly, "I was just thinking that when I die, I want to be right here."

Her expression tightened. "What?"

He touched the fine line drawn between her eyes. "Shh. I wasn't talking about…" He kissed her quickly and fiercely, then drew back. "Love, I'm fine. I'm not perfect. The therapist didn't promise perfection. But I'm better." He motioned to the closed doors on the far side of the room. "Look, the doors are closed."

"Yes, they are." He could feel her relaxing as he spoke.

"We're in the Bliss Hotel, in the room where we first made love, and it's our honeymoon." He laughed and it felt good. "If Wally and Emma manage to leave us alone long enough, we'll make this a very memorable honeymoon."

Her smile touched his soul. "It's pretty wonderful, isn't it?"

"It's beyond that. Six months ago I wouldn't have given a tinker's damn for my life, and now..." He could barely say the words. "I have a life. God, have I got a life."

Her hand settled over his heart. "We're so lucky."

He shifted so he was facing her in the bed, his hand resting on the curve of her hip. "Either lucky or blessed, maybe both."

"Definitely," she whispered.

Her fingertips touched the pulse that beat at the base of his throat. "I wish things could have been different...for others."

He knew she meant the ambassador. The man had been dead since he'd been taken. But he accepted the fact there wasn't anything either one of them could have done. And in someway, meeting Whitney and finding his life again seemed to balance out some of the bad. "Life isn't perfect," he whispered as he touched her lips with his. "Life's barely fair at times." He tasted her skin along the sweep of her jaw. "But I'm not questioning it right now."

She curled her leg around his thigh and pressed her hips to his. "Neither am I."

The kiss was long and deep and, in some indefinable way, a binding of their lives, a seal of some sort. Jake didn't understand it, not any more than he understood what brought Whitney into his life when he needed her. He just accepted it. "Tomorrow we'll go up to the burial grounds after Emma makes the big Christmas dinner that she's been talking about all day."

"Yes, tomorrow," she whispered as her hand skimmed over his stomach, following the path of hair on his skin. "And we'll take the van so we make sure we get stuck up there for a good long time."

He laughed at that, but the sound was unsteady as she found him and surrounded him with her heat. "I don't think we need that excuse anymore. We could stay until the morning if we wanted to."

With an ease that made Jake feel as if he and Whitney had been together for a lifetime, she was over him and shifted until he was in her, deep and sure. "Yes, until morning," he whispered as she began to move.

He shuddered at the jolt of pure pleasure that coursed through him, then his own rhythm matched hers. And as the ecstasy took over, as the pleasure of this woman with him became a part of his soul, Jake finally knew he wasn't alone. That two could really become one.

*   *   *   *   *

HE'S AN

AMERICAN HERO

Men of mettle. Men of integrity. Real men who know the real meaning of love. Each month, Intimate Moments salutes these true American Heroes.

For July: THAT SAME OLD FEELING,
by Judith Duncan.
Chase McCall had come home a new man. Yet old lover Devon Manyfeathers soon stirred familiar feelings—and renewed desire.

For August: MICHAEL'S GIFT,
by Marilyn Pappano.
Michael Bennett knew his visions prophesied certain death. Yet he would move the high heavens to change beautiful Valery Navarre's fate.

For September: DEFENDER,
by Kathleen Eagle.
Gideon Defender had reformed his bad-boy ways to become a leader among his people. Yet one habit—loving Raina McKenny—had never died, especially after Gideon learned she'd returned home.

AMERICAN HEROES: Men who give all they've got for their country, their work—the women they love.

Only from

Take 4 bestselling love stories FREE

Plus get a FREE surprise gift!

Special Limited-time Offer

Mail to Silhouette Reader Service™

3010 Walden Avenue
P.O. Box 1867
Buffalo, N.Y. 14269-1867

YES! Please send me 4 free Silhouette Intimate Moments® novels and my free surprise gift. Then send me 6 brand-new novels every month, which I will receive months before they appear in bookstores. Bill me at the low price of $2.89 each plus 25¢ delivery and applicable sales tax, if any.* That's the complete price and—compared to the cover prices of $3.50 each—quite a bargain! I understand that accepting the books and gift places me under no obligation ever to buy any books. I can always return a shipment and cancel at any time. Even if I never buy another book from Silhouette, the 4 free books and the surprise gift are mine to keep forever.

245 BPA ANRR

Name	(PLEASE PRINT)	
Address	Apt. No.	
City	State	Zip

This offer is limited to one order per household and not valid to present Silhouette Intimate Moments® subscribers. *Terms and prices are subject to change without notice. Sales tax applicable in N.Y.

UMOM-94R   ©1990 Harlequin Enterprises Limited

explores the dark side of love....

Join award-winning author Rachel Lee as

Rachel Lee will tingle your senses in August when she visits the dark side of love in her latest Conard County title, **THUNDER MOUNTAIN, SS #37.**

For years, Gray Cloud had guarded his beloved Thunder Mountain, protecting its secrets and mystical powers from human exploitation. Then came Mercy Kendrick.... But someone—or something—wanted her dead. Alone with the tempestuous forces of nature, Mercy turned to Gray Cloud, only to find a storm of a very different kind raging in his eyes. Look for their terrifying tale, only from Silhouette Shadows.

ROMANTIC TRADITIONS

Barbara Faith heats up **ROMANTIC TRADITIONS** in July with **DESERT MAN, IM #578**, featuring the forever-sultry sheikh plot line.

Josie McCall knew better than to get involved with Sheikh Kumar Ben Ari. Worlds apart in thought and custom, both suspected their love was destined for failure. Then a tribal war began, and Josie faced the grim possibility of losing her desert lover—for good.

October 1994 will feature Justine Davis's **LEFT AT THE ALTAR**, her timely take on the classic story line of the same name. And remember, **ROMANTIC TRADITIONS** will continue to bring you the best-loved plot lines from your most-cherished authors, so don't miss any of them— only in **INTIMATE MOMENTS®** *Silhouette®*

SILHOUETTE INTIMATE MOMENTS®

WIDE OPEN SPACES

Return to Southern Alberta's rustic ranch land as Judith Duncan's Wide Open Spaces miniseries continues in July with THAT SAME OLD FEELING, IM#577.

Chase McCall had come home a new man. Yet painful memories—and an old but familiar lover—awaited his return. Devon Manyfeathers had refused him once, but one look into her soulful brown eyes had Chance focusing on forever.

And there will be more McCalls to meet in future months, as they learn love's lessons in the wide open spaces of Western Canada.

It's those rambunctious Rawlings brothers again!
You met Gable and Cooper Rawlings in IM #523
and IM #553. Now meet their youngest brother,
Flynn Rawlings, in

by Linda Turner

Fun-loving rodeo cowboy Flynn Rawlings
couldn't believe it. From the moment he'd
approached beautiful barrel racer Tate Baxter,
she'd been intent on freezing him out. But Tate
was the woman he'd been waiting for all his life,
and he wasn't about to take no for an answer!

Don't miss FLYNN (IM #572), available in June.
And look for his sister, Kat's, story as
Linda Turner's thrilling saga concludes in

THE WILD WEST

Coming to you throughout 1994...only from
Silhouette Intimate Moments.